D0107363

Floyd Harbor

Floyd Harbor

Stories

Joel Mowdy

Catapult  New York

Copyright © 2019 by Joel Mowdy
First published in the United States in 2019 by Catapult (catapult.co)
All rights reserved

ISBN: 978-1-948226-11-0

Jacket design by Jaya Miceli
Book design by Wah-Ming Chang

Catapult titles are distributed to the trade by Publishers Group West
Phone: 866-400-5351

Library of Congress Control Number: 2018956397

Printed in the United States of America
10 9 8 7 6 5 4 3 2 1

For Semka and Z

Contents

Floyd Harbor

Salty's

‖‖‖‖‖‖‖‖‖‖‖‖‖‖‖‖‖‖‖‖‖‖‖‖‖‖‖‖

The bungalows on Neighborhood Road, Mastic Beach, had been summer homes, Fire Island a short drive from there via the Smith Point Bridge. Now bicycles built from parts huddled under lock and chain along the concrete stoop of Paul's Bicycle & Shoe Repair. Their wheels caught clumps of dead leaves in the wind. Baskets of doll heads collected dust among spools of thread and balls of yarn in the neighboring unmarked craft store, where bundles of cotton had been stacked like sandbags in the window display.

Across the street was the bungalow turned into Sweet Magic, its window featuring Maltos, Neccos, Mary Janes, Dum-Dums, Lemon Heads, Fortune Bubbles, Newports, Winchesters, and Marlboros. Oily spots told where kids had pressed their faces and cupped their hands to see inside. Then Sweet Magic closed its doors, the displays disappeared, the sign was vandalized and removed, the window broken and boarded up. Now stalks of thin bamboo bound together were makeshift palm trees, attached to the front of the new store with wire and nails. They reached from the ground to the roof, and leaves made with the tips of cattails and corn husks were stapled flush to the wall near the bottom edge of the rain gutter. The new window was painted blue. The canopy over the steps was thatched river grass. On the front of the canopy hung a sign the size of a license plate that said SALTY'S.

Will kissed Carla Brown right there. For a moment, he was somewhere else.

"What is this place?" she said.

"It's Salty's," Will said. "No one knows what it is."

Dorian, his roommate, wasn't home. Headlights threw shadows through the blinds and across Carla. Will kissed her ear and smelled her hair, then kissed her neck where a swirling cowlick hid. He unbuttoned her shirt and pricked his finger on her drugstore name tag. He could taste his pot and beer breath on her breast, her workday in the stubble in her armpit. She laughed when he kissed her there, but then moaned and said, "Come here," even though he was on top of her already.

"Here," she said, reaching into her pocketbook on the floor. She pulled out something small and plastic.

"Condom?" he said.

"Meth."

This was the year before Will walked upon the scene of a naked young man, in the early morning sun, fending off a team of police at the USA gas station. The man was hard to catch, and he didn't seem to understand what world he was in. He thought he was a fish and needed to get back in the water. He broke out of the plastic ties, so the police resorted to using real cuffs on the man's sandy ankles, too. He floundered in the backseat of the cruiser. He had been on the high school basketball team.

A commercial for a Long Island college was playing. "Stay close," it said. "Go far." Will switched to the cartoon channel. He watched an annoying commercial for lollipops and turned the TV off when a show for babies came on. It was time for work.

The bowling alley was on William Floyd Parkway, about a mile south of Sunrise Highway. The bowling lanes were empty. Will scraped gum and taxi stickers off the pay phones. Later, when the lanes filled with league play, he swept up spilled ashtrays, restocked the bathroom, collected beer bottles, and walked between the gutters to pick up dead wood. Dead wood was a pin knocked out of reach of the sweeper, lost in the gutter. At the end of his shift, he carried trash to the Dumpsters in the parking lot, where on breaks he smoked to the rumble and flush of bowling on the other side of the wall. Soon he'd see Carla at the super drugstore in the neighboring strip mall, between King Kullen and New Rooster.

"Is there a hero in you?" the voice on television said.

Dorian was discussing a proposition to make money. The scheme had to do with mattresses. Will lost the thread of Dorian's pitch due to the joint they'd smoked. The army commercial was reminding him of the time he'd almost enlisted. He'd gone through with his physical, but he wasn't home the morning the recruiter came to collect him for swearing in. The baby Rebecca was pregnant with wasn't his. He'd lost any reason to cling to a sense of duty.

"Are you in?" Dorian said. "We'll split it three ways. You, me, and the guy with the van."

"I don't understand. Say it again?"

"It's simple. You pay for the mattress, the guy drives to the other store, I return it, we split the profit."

Will had questions. "Where does the profit come from?"

"Because you switch the tags," Dorian said. "Are you listening? Remember that mattress I had before I got the futon? Like, right before?" When Dorian bought the mattress at Cody's on Montauk Highway in Floyd Harbor, he had switched the price code with that of a smaller down-market mattress half the price. He was giving himself a discount. That wasn't unusual. But then someone gave Dorian the futon, so he returned the mattress, but to a different Cody's because the friend with the van was going there, and that other Cody's accepted the returned mattress because of Cody's unique return policy. Any product exclusive to Cody's collection could be returned for a full refund at any Cody's without a receipt, if it was still in its original package.

It was the full refund Dorian wasn't expecting. He'd paid a lot less for the mattress than the bundle of cash he got back for it. He and the driver tried again that next Saturday. He returned that mattress to the next-nearest Cody's, in Bellport. Full refund. On Sunday, he tried two more mattresses, which meant switching two tags. That part went fine. Then they had lunch at the pizzeria two stores down, and then tried returning the mattresses to the same Cody's afterward, thinking it would save on gas.

The woman working customer service punched in the mattress code. "Is that what these things cost?" she said when the price appeared. She reentered the code, getting the same result. She was the employee who had rung up Dorian earlier. Something was almost clicking for her. Dorian was lucky she didn't feel the urge to look further into the discrepancy.

"So, I can't do phase one on this again," Dorian said. "The risk is too high."

"And you want me to take the risk?" Will said. "No way."

"Switching tags is your game, Will. This is easy for you."

"On socks and shirts. Deodorant. A few dollars. You almost got caught flipping mattresses."

Besides the difference in scale, Will had restricted his

game to the super drugstore on William Floyd Parkway, and only when Carla Brown was working. He would switch tags, she would ring him up. Their scheme was tight.

The Caprice Classic looked white or yellow in the dawn. Where would Will go if this car ran? Where would he drive if it were his? He'd never been anywhere. An old white-and-blue bumper sticker attached to the dashboard asked: WHERE'S DA HARBOR?

"What are you thinking?" Carla said.

"I'm not really thinking anything."

"I watched you sleep last time," Carla said.

"You watched me sleep?"

"You didn't look like you were sleeping. You looked like you were thinking with your eyes closed."

"I was probably thinking about you."

She smiled. "Sweet. But what else do you think about?"

"Why can't we go inside your house?"

"The house is off limits. That's all. Ask me something else."

"Tell me about when you were in rehab."

She was quiet for a moment. "Madonna Heights is all girls. There was this one thing at night in the summer. Some guys from around would sneak through the woods behind the grounds and just, like, hang around by the fence. They would try to look in the windows from there and—I don't know—see what they could see. Their cigarettes glowed in the dark at lights out. They would just sit there, you know, as if the counselors were just gonna let us out and have sex with them all. I don't know." She stopped picking at the hole in the car seat. "What's the worst thing you ever did for money?"

"I work in a bowling alley."

"I'm being serious," she said.

"So am I. Why? What about you?" Will said. "What did you do?"

"I fucked once."

"Oh, yeah?" Will said.

She kept a straight face. Will looked away.

"It wasn't like it seems," she said. "I knew him. I went to school with him."

"Oh." Will looked down the street through the windshield. There was a tiny crack like a spider's thread.

"We were going to hook up one time but . . . Well, we didn't that time. And then this time, yes."

She was pale, and from that angle her cheeks were sunk in. Did she offer herself to the guy, or did he ask?

"You went to your father's house for a few days?"

"I told you that on the phone."

"I know, so what did you do?"

"I'm not saying anything, Will. I'm just telling you something that happened once, like one time. I'm not, like, telling you anything recent."

"I didn't say you were telling me anything. Just something that happened one time."

"I guess I shouldn't be telling you this at all."

"No, it's okay. Tell me everything."

Something inside her rattled when she breathed in. "That was, I don't know, the lowest point." She blinked and there were tears. She put her hand over her mouth to hide the broken tooth. "God, what's wrong with me?"

Will put his arms around her and held her hands. "It's okay," he said into the top of her head. Carla's body was stiff, her arms tight to her sides. Will wanted to go. He wanted to walk home and forget about her, but he couldn't just get up and leave her, either. Soon she turned herself over, burying her head into Will's lap. He stroked her hair. He ran his fingers through her curls until she fell asleep. Shadows in the woods softened. Birds chirped. Light bent around the crack in the windshield. He left her in the car and walked home.

"It's like I see these people at the bowling alley, and they get excited about bowling. I mean, what else do they do? They go home and think about the next time they're going bowling. They dream about bowling a perfect game. Probably. I don't know. Maybe I don't know what I'm talking about, but it's just a feeling I have with people sometimes. You know, not just them but everybody. Like people who work a job and—and they do their job, and then maybe they'll get a better job. Or they dream about making manager someday. Or even people like the guy at Handy Pantry looking for handouts, waiting for something—I don't know what for. I look at them—all these people—and they're all the same. They get into these things in their lives, and that's who they are. I just don't want to be like that. You know what I'm talking about?"

Dorian was kicking Will's ass in Backstreet Fight. "Did we order food yet?" He had been out raving for two days and still wore a pacifier on a necklace of plastic rainbow beads. Dorian had been a jock in high school, then a skater punk working as a bowling alley mechanic. He quit that job and tidied his facial hair into the outline of a beard, bought some colorful shirts, a pair of baggy overalls.

"But do you know what I'm talking about?" Will said.

A city of smokestacks loomed in the screen's background. Will played best when using Sumo Wrestler, but he was no match for either Dorian or the system whatever fighter he chose, or whichever buttons he pressed in whatever order—a strategy that made Will's character flip or whip out power chops that he couldn't repeat. Anyway, those moves were always blocked and used against him. Kung Fu Master caught his Sumo Wrestler's fist, spun him around, lifted him, and slammed him down to the pavement. Will tried to roll back onto his feet, but Kung Fu Master's jackhammer leg stomped his head into a puddle of pixels the colors of blood and bone.

"You never answered me about the mattresses," Dorian said.

"We already talked about that. I'm not in."

"I don't know what you're afraid of," he said.

"Getting arrested," Will said. "Going to jail."

There was a knock on the door.

"No one's going to jail." Dorian answered the door. It was pizza from down the street. He gave the delivery kid a little plastic baggie as payment.

"Was that ecstasy?"

"Why?" Dorian said. "Do you want to buy some?"

The next round had begun.

Puddles froze into sheets of white ice. Take-out containers cluttered the kitchen area. Dorian slept on the futon. Will played the new video games. When Dorian woke up, he watched Will lose a boxing match. Will offered the control.

"I'm going to start charging rent on games," Dorian said. He took the control. "What happened to that girl you were seeing?"

"We're taking a break," Will said.

"She got any friends?"

"I'll ask if she knows anyone."

"I have a girl," Dorian said. "That's why I'm out all the time. I just want to know if she's a loner like you."

Later, Dorian went out, and Will played until level five. Then he walked around Carla's block a bunch of times. He wasn't dressed for the cold. He went home and lost three rounds of solitaire. He put the cards in order. He dialed Rebecca and hung up on the first ring.

Then he put the ecstasy he'd bought from Dorian in his pocket and went out.

When she was sleeping, Carla's cheeks twitched as though tiny shocks were crawling under her skin. The sky was pink and blue. Will lit a cigarette and held it close to the sliver in the car window. A breeze sucked the smoke into the cold.

Dorian sat on their concrete step with one hand in his pocket, the other holding a cigarette.

"What are you doing out here?" Will said. The owner of the smoke shop rolled the shield from his window.

Doran pointed to Salty's. "What is that place?"

"I don't know," Will said. "No one knows what it is. Are you going inside?"

"I'm waiting here a minute," Dorian said.

Will went into their apartment and microwaved instant coffee. Dorian disappeared from the step.

It was the Christmas season, a Saturday night. People got off from their jobs and kids got off from school. They needed something to do. There was a disc jockey. There were bowling prizes to hand out. A blizzard had begun. Three inches already covered the ground. Will gave out red strike tickets and picked up dead wood while pop blared through the speakers and high school kids posed and joked in the arcade room.

Then he saw Rebecca in lane three with the father of the kid, but no kid. The kid was probably home with a babysitter. Rebecca wore the blue jeans Will had bought her for her birthday two years earlier. She still fit inside them. She dropped a gutter ball, shrugged, and turned around. Her teammates cheered her. She smiled at them.

Carla slept with the light on. She had snuck Will through the basement bedroom window. The room was warmed by an electric heater, but so dank the pink drywall had spots of mold that split and puckered the paint like wet, parting lips. She slept naked under a blue comforter, her hair spread out across her pillow. She smelled of cigarettes, but she was young, and the broken tooth was farther back in her mouth where he couldn't see.

On the floor Will found his pants next to her blue apron, his shirt under the bed.

The world had turned to white and gray. The water was dark in the creek and the bay, the bay lined with large chunks of ice the color of the moon. Glassy ice floated in the water, spreading out from the shore of Mastic Beach to the shore of Fire Island. The horizon blended with a gray windy sky that thrust against the trees. Streets flooded with slush a shade of blue he'd seen only in dreams.

He was bundled in layers that restricted movement and saw the world through the fuzzy slit of a scarf wrapped up to his eyes, a hat pulled over his brow. There were no other people. The houses had been vacated with the flood warning. Forward through slush, Ducky Lane turned into a dirt road where the creek met the bay, where houses were built on stilts in case something like this storm should happen. Private docks lining the mouth of the bay had been uprooted, and they jutted out of the water obtusely, crooked planks and railings covered in gleaming ice. This wasn't the flimsy snow of past winters. It wasn't smeared into grime on the side of the road. This snow had taken control.

The bay had swallowed Ducky Lane where it curved out of the creek and became Riviera Drive, so Will walked through backyards where the slush came up to his knees. The cold water stung his legs. He passed under the homes on stilts, treaded through a flooded field of cattails, and emerged on Cranberry Drive into more slush, a half-mile from his apartment. Snow flew sideways under the yellow streetlights like flecks of gold and blew off branches in chunks the size of bowling balls. Then the wind died. Will was inside a void, insulated with cotton, sterilized by the cold. It was a space with neither time nor memory. A space to empty himself into, but there was nobody there to listen. He wanted to be home and warm. He imagined living with

Carla on a bed under blankets with all this snow outside turning everything into white plush.

At the apartment, Dorian's stuff was packed by the door. His friend with the van had already picked up the futon. He was moving out, going half/half on a new place with someone named Grady.

Carla disappeared the next day. She wasn't working at the drugstore. At her house, her mother told Will not to come looking anymore. It took two more weeks to find out that she was back in rehab. He rode the public bus across Suffolk County to the mall and then walked down backstreets and through woods to the fence that divided Madonna Heights from the rest of the world. The snow in the woods was still untouched. When Will stepped on its icy crust, it held his weight for a moment before breaking through to soft snow underneath. The sun was going down. He crouched against the fence and looked at the glowing windows of the stout, unfriendly building. His fingers were numb from the cold, from holding a cigarette. He wondered if the boys Carla talked about would show up, the ones who loitered along the fence. Maybe it was a summer thing for them. Maybe they grew out of it. Maybe they decided it was a waste of time. Will waited for the lights to go off so that Carla could see the glowing cherry of his cigarette and know it was Will she could barely make out in the shadows. He waited all night for some sign, some acknowledgment of his presence, but all that happened was the lights went down and he was alone in the dark with two matches and a quarter-pack of cigarettes.

In two years, he'd have been out of the army if he'd gone. Empty beer cans lined the edge of the coffee table. He reached for his cigarettes. The pack was empty. The stores were closed. The phone was ringing. Will was supposed to be at work. He walked next door to use the cigarette machine at Schultzie's. The bouncer wouldn't let him.

"Come on," Will said. "Greta's my landlady. I live right there."

"Listen, buddy," the bouncer said, "I can smell the alcohol on you. You're underage. I'll throw you out on your ass, you try to come in here."

Will walked away, quietly cursing the bouncer. He stopped in front of Salty's. The washed-up tropical beach hut covered in crusty snow sat back on the sidewalk in the center of the village business district. Will tried looking through the blue display window with his hands cupped to the glass. The paint was too thick. The doorknob wouldn't turn. He went back to the apartment and the ringing phone. It was time to quit.

"Hello?"

"I need you to bail me out," Dorian said.

"What are you talking about? The mattresses?"

"What?" Dorian said, incredulous. Then he whispered, "Don't talk like that on the phone, dick. You have to bail me out."

"You're in jail?"

"Fucking Christ, man, are you listening to me?"

The phone went dead. Will sat on the kitchen chair with the receiver in his hand. He straightened a cigarette butt from the ashtray and lit it. Then he dialed her number.

"Who's this?" Rebecca said.

"How's the baby?"

"Who is this?"

"It's me, Will."

"Will? What do you want?"

"Nothing. I don't want anything."

Rebecca hung up.

Will closed his eyes. Music hummed from the bar on the other side of his wall.

It had been early spring, a Sunday. Rebecca's parents and little sisters had taken the hatchback on a daylong shopping trip. Will's and Rebecca's clothes were on the kitchen floor. A feel-good movie played on the television in the master bedroom. Sunlight poured through the open sliding door to the back deck. Rebecca, naked and sleepy under her parents' bedspread, had fit herself against Will, her breath on his neck, her hand on his chest. "This is the way it's going to be," she said.

Was she talking about the movie, or the moment they were in? It was all the same. He kissed her forehead, held her tighter, and disappeared with her under the covers.

Golden

||||||||||||||||||||||||||||||||||||||||||||||

One summer I dyed my brown hair blond and combed it in a Caesar style, and I roasted in a tanning bed twice a week, twenty minutes at a time, cooking perfectly around like a rotisserie chicken. I owned three identical white silk shirts and blue jeans that hugged my ass, the legs gradually widening so that only my toes sticking out of leather sandals showed at the selvage. I clasped the two buttons at the top of the shirt and left the rest open.

Oryn thought it was sexy that way. He gelled his hair back and wore only black except for his socks and undershirts, which were matching pastels that splintered from the bottom of his pant legs and over his collar. He'd dropped out of FIT when he landed a job with this company that designed and manufactured caps for toiletries, from shampoo bottles to aftershave, including big-ticket fragrances from the same designers of his wardrobe. He had an office on Fifth Avenue, leased a lofty apartment in Astoria, and on a whim dropped a few thousand dollars on a new sofa that became my favorite place to sleep. I loved it while it lasted.

Before Oryn, I'd knock on James's door in the dorms and say, "Come out, shit-head, let's play the game." We'd hit the bars along the Long Island Rail Road in search of an easy target, a fatty or a butter face. ("She has a nice body, but her . . .") I had James on looks, but he could get her to trust him. He'd look her in the eyes. He took her by the arm with a hand on her back, told her to watch her step as he guided her around the pile of broken glass that had been a drunk sophomore's bottle of beer, tell the sophomore to give up his stool for the lady. He borrowed the broom and dustpan from the barman to sweep up the shards and resumed talking to Kim, standing by her, gesticulating and looking her in the eyes.

Then I walked over from across the bar.

"Jared," James said, "you have to meet Kim. Kimberly, this is Jared."

I leaned in close to her. "What's your name, Kim?"

Kim had been considering James. Maybe she'd imagined waking to him in sunlight under crisp, bleached sheets, but then I came along, so she felt guilty for getting his hopes up. Now she had to let him down. (Girls like that know how it feels—happens to them all the time.) In the same stroke, she didn't want to lose the prize, which was me.

I wanted to buy her a drink and I was holding my and James's money, or I thought I was. Someone had lifted my wallet. This sucked for everyone because we had only had one drink apiece so far. Kim felt sorry and offered to buy me one. She offered James a drink, too, because she didn't want to make him a third wheel—she knew how that felt. The girlfriend she had come with had left with her boyfriend an hour earlier.

We ran out of cigarettes. Kim bought us a pack. She bought rounds and we toasted her every time, me slipping my arm around her waist and sliding her quarters into the slot on the pool table, James caressing her hand, both of us talking her into taking us to breakfast when the sun came up, fretting about the train fare going home, and digging into her backseat for change while she got out to pump gas into her hatchback.

I had Kim in her car while James smoked in the train station parking lot. Another time, James hooked up with the girl.

Once, we shared a girl in her dorm room.

Everybody won. James and I got a night out. The girl got to feel like a princess. Sure, she probably felt duped when she called the number I gave her and got a Pizza Hut, but for one night in her sorry young life she felt like gold.

———

Once, I was in love. It lasted four years. I thought I was in love three times, but the last time told me the other times were a joke. Her name was Shelly. She had freckles, and black hair like those women in shampoo commercials. It was the kind of hair a girl could wrap up in a sloppy bun or tie into a loose ponytail, and it was always perfect. The holes in the knees of her favorite jeans were perfect, too. She made me feel like I could do anything I wanted if I set my mind to it, that I could do so much better than working in restaurants out east. That was what I did before Shelly. I started as a dishwasher in the Hamptons and had worked my way through salad boy and line cook, teetering on the edge of sous chef. Shelly was the reason I went to Suffolk Community College and then transferred to a university close to hers in Nassau County when she graduated high school.

"We're going to be poor," I told her. We were lying in the darkness of her bedroom. We were talking about university, about how we could survive for a few years on student loans and state aid. Too many girls she used to be friends with had dropped out of high school. Her sister got married and became a mother right after graduation. And then there was this girl Rebecca, Shelly's best friend in middle school, who would graduate high school with a baby in her arms, a few contenders for the role of father. Shelly wanted something better for herself. Her family wanted better for her.

Her father sold the boat he'd saved up for to help pay her first-semester tuition.

"Can you handle being poor until we have degrees?" I said.

Yes, she could.

But in the weeks before she broke up with me, Shelly complained that I never took her out anywhere. A few days later, walking back from the diner down the street from her college, she said her feet hurt and she wondered out loud why everyone had a car except for us. Only days after that, her friend from acting class squealed about a bracelet her boyfriend had bought her, and Shelly threw me this look like I had done something wrong. She had to be massaged, the lights off, her radio set on some slow jazz with the volume low so the singer sounded nailed inside a box somewhere far away. She spread a bath towel over the sheets to keep them clean. Then she had headaches all the time, menstrual cramps. Then she just didn't feel like sex. She wasn't in the mood.

"You don't do anything romantic," she said two days before she broke up with me. We were lying in her bed, watching Oprah. She always wanted me to watch Oprah with her.

"Yes, I do," I said.

"Like what? Can you name even one time?"

"That time I walked into Hempstead at three in the morning to get you Nyquil. You were sick. You couldn't sleep, remember?"

"That's not romantic, Jared. That's standard."

"Hempstead," I said, "at night. It's a bad neighborhood. You want me to die for you?"

She took the remote, flicked through channels. "No, just something different."

Four years together ended on a cold October night at the start of my junior year. Wind tore the leaves off the trees outside her window. She was too young to be so serious, she said. Pacing her floor between the closet and the door, Shelly sitting on the bed and crying and holding out to me the silver promise ring I'd given her, I looked back to three weeks before and saw it coming. I was too frustrated to unpack the slow, plotted route she'd taken to sever herself from me—too choked with disbelief that it was happening now.

"I guess I'll see you around," I said. I slammed the door behind me. Then I stood in the hallway, waiting for her to come looking for me, but after a long time nothing happened.

One night, about a month later, I saw Shelly in front of her dorm building. The parking lot had just been repaved. She clicked in heels to the passenger side of a black Lexus with tinted windows. Her dress was flimsy black. Her pale cheeks were colored with blush. She never wore blush.

I found a job at a Greek restaurant after Shelly dumped me. Craig, the manager, was in his thirties. On Sunday nights, after closing, when the boss left, Craig and I sat at the bar and had a few drinks. Conversations turned to sex if they went on long enough. I told him that Shelly had been a virgin and I'd had to be patient with her, but she came around eventually, opened to me, even asked me to spank her a few times. He told me about his lady (that's what he called her) and how he'd watched her jerk off a stranger in a dark corner at a nightclub.

"I don't care what anybody says," Craig said one night. "The ass is full of nerve endings. It's supposed to feel good. The toughest guy will admit that taking a shit feels good. It doesn't mean he's gay, just human. What's wrong with a finger? What's wrong with two fingers if it feels good?"

I nodded, sipped my beer. The top three buttons of his shirt had come undone over the last three drinks. The lights above the bar were dim and the liquor bottles glowed like church windows at sunset.

Craig fixed his eyes on me, leaned in a little. "I'm not ashamed to say that. Play with my prostate. Massage my anus."

"There's nothing wrong with it," I said. I remembered when Shelly started loosening up in the bedroom, finally touched my balls, and before long I could talk her into grabbing anything—her hairbrush—and pushing the handle against my ass just as I was about to come. When she did this, I could imagine a hard penis pushing against me—an organ detached from anything human, like a rubber dildo, yet at the same time having the human capability to take pleasure in me offering myself to it.

Craig said, "Do you need to label yourself just because something feels good?"

"No." And right then, I knew what would happen. "If it feels good, just go with it."

His face was relaxed, his mouth slightly open. I could see his tongue pushing against the back of his teeth.

In the daytime, I sliced strips off a thick tube of gyro meat. First, I would slide a poker into the cylinder-shaped meat, and then it went into this vertical rotisserie that sent waves of heat into my face as I worked the knife along the side, shaving quarter-inch-thick lengths from the top to the bottom. Juice dripped from the meat and collected into a puddle at the base of the rotisserie. I jerked the knife back and forth. Back and forth. It was sweaty work.

If I had the chance, I would step out the back door to cool off, stick my hands in the snow if there was any around.

I met James in the bathroom of our second-floor dorm that December, a few weeks before I quit my job at the restaurant. I was back from work and had just finished showering. When I opened the curtain to the stall, James was lying on the floor. He had an openmouthed smile and his head slowly moved from side to side, his long hair fanned out behind him. I'd seen him before on those restless nights when I'd pace in my room, smoking cigarettes, writing crappy love sonnets on a whiteboard with my red dry-erase marker, counting the syllables with my fingers. I had a habit of peering through the spyglass on the door whenever I walked by it, as if I was expecting to see something in the hallway.

Something to take me away.

A few times, way past two in the morning, I saw James unlock his door.

Lying on the bathroom tiles, he said, "Hey, you live on this floor."

He smelled like wet cigarettes and beer, a hint of cologne. I stood in the shower stall in my towel, my hand still on the open curtain. "Yeah," I said, "I live in two-sixteen. You live in two-thirteen."

"Yeah," he said, still smiling and almost laughing to himself. "Dude, you should come out some night."

"Yeah, I will. Sure. Sometime." I stepped over him and walked out of the bathroom, not yet knowing his name.

I saw him again the next day, Saturday. I was tired of my job. I called in sick and figured I would get some reading done for psychology. I had to leave my room to do this. When I stayed in my room for too long I turned into a mad poet, my detachment from Shelly spilling out ugly onto my whiteboard.

James called from beyond the door. "Dude from the shower, come out tonight."

I didn't think he would remember. "Hey," I said through the door, "listen, I'm flat broke, man. I get paid every other Friday, so if you catch me next Friday—"

"Don't be a shit-head. Come out. We don't need money."

I didn't see Craig again after I quit the restaurant. James would call or stop by my dorm room to see if I wanted to play the game. Mostly I was good to go, but sometimes I just didn't feel like kissing up to some dog. I wanted someone to kiss up to me. I wanted to do something I wasn't supposed to do, just for a night, and then I'd be good for weeks.

I hit the Bunkhouse. I could feel the men looking at me: skinny boy-faced men in their silver V-neck shirts, queens, bashful young ones out looking for the first time. There were always the guys looking for love, dressed in a polo shirt or knitted sweater; these men were tired of the scene. They had disillusionment stamped in their faces. They complained into their drinks that all anyone wanted was a random fuck. I stayed clear of them.

An older man in an expensive suit sat at the bar, nodding his head to the music and scanning the crowd. A gold watch peeked out from under the cuff of his jacket. He was a vulture, looking to impress a stringy-muscled boy—any one of them—as they came off the dance floor to wedge between the barstools for a drink. The boys were like me, except I wasn't going to end up someone's bitch. The suit could buy me all the drinks he wanted, but I was more like him than some gold-digging pretty boy.

My summer with Oryn started out like this: a lingering glance, a smile, a casual trip to his car in the parking lot. It was near the end of my junior year, and I had withdrawn from all my classes—dropped out, according to the school. I had no plans, no job. I had nowhere to go except home, and who wants to go there, admitting defeat? I sold my stereo and my computer and spent most nights crashing in James's dorm room, where I kept my stuff in bags on the floor of his closet. Some weekend nights I'd go home with some butter face, or I'd make it down to the Bunkhouse and hook up, spend a night in a motel room at someone else's expense. But the semester was coming to an end, and James's dorm room wasn't going to be an option anymore.

"Do you want to go to my apartment?" Oryn said as we left the Bunkhouse.

I thought about it on the short walk to his car. Waking up next to a man in his apartment: what was that like?

"I live in Astoria, but I can give you money to take the train home in the morning. I can drive you home in the morning."

I spent the night, the next night, and came back a week later because Oryn had tickets to Porno for Pyros at Roseland. My things moved from James's dorm room to Oryn's apartment. Soon there was an empty drawer for my underwear.

———

I imagined the other clients dreamed about the beach while lying in their tanning beds, wearing Speedos or nothing and those little eye protectors while bright heat emitted from bulbs inches from their skin, but I saw only black with flashes of white, like a freshly paved wet parking lot, its shallow puddles reflecting light from a streetlamp, or a girl in black in the same desolate parking lot, her skin and her string of pearls standing out in the darkness.

After twenty minutes, my skin felt tight. I stepped out and looked back at the bed. I could imagine myself lying inside, even rotating while my body turned gold to match the color of my dyed yellow hair. The thought made me dizzy. Back at the apartment, all was quiet except for the humming of the air conditioner. This belonged to me until Oryn came home. I stripped and lay on the cool white sofa, my sweat drying to my skin. Oryn would find me sleeping there when he came home from work, the result of his romantic gestures blond and broiled.

According to Shelly, I had been romantic twice. The first time was on our one-year anniversary, November 17. Her mother was out of town visiting relatives, her father was at work, and Shelly was at school all day. I decided I would let myself in and surprise her with a hot candle-lit bubble bath, ready to dip into when she came in from the cold. I cleaned the bathroom. I set up candles on the sink, put a radio on the toilet seat, and found a station playing smooth jazz that floated like steam around the shower curtain. But when I went to fill the tub half an hour before she was to get home, all that came out of the faucet was freezing water. By the time she showed up, I had four huge pots of water heating on the range top and four potfuls already dumped into the tub.

The second time was the following summer. It was blazing hot for over a week, and when I came to Shelly's house from my line-cook job at night she would moan and wheeze with a damp washcloth on her forehead. On one particularly boiling night she sat up crying in the dark because she felt as though she were suffocating. I told her to get dressed. We sneaked her out the window and walked to a motel on the highway that had air-conditioning.

In early August, when I had just gotten back from tanning and getting my roots bleached, Oryn came home with a big cardboard box. He carried it into the living room, where I lounged on the sofa in my boxers, watching *Kids in the Hall* reruns.

"I got you something," he said. He put the box on the coffee table. "Guess what it is."

"A silk shirt." He had gotten me three by this time, and the last time I had offended him when I didn't act surprised.

"Come on, be serious."

I stretched my leg out to the coffee table and tapped the box with my foot to estimate its weight. The box was heavy. He always brought home samples of shampoo and fragrances that the company gave away. I thought the gift might be that, and I said so.

"No, why would I give you that as a gift? It's something else. Something you said you wanted."

I didn't remember asking for anything. "I give up," I said.

He opened the box. There were half-used tubes of acrylics and oils, brushes, watercolors, a little bottle of paint thinner, a small palette, and some other painting supplies.

He said, "I know this retired professor who used to teach art history at NYU, and he paints too, and now he's writing a book on interior design—but anyway, he was getting rid of some old supplies his partner left behind. He said I could have them, so I brought them home for you."

"That's nice," I said. "Thank you."

Oryn seemed disappointed. "You know, that one day when you said you might want to take up painting? That day we were watching that painting show?"

Then I remembered. It was my first week living with Oryn and we were watching Bob Ross paint a landscape on PBS. Oryn leaned in toward me, slowly got his hand under my shirt, and started rubbing my side with the backs of his fingers. He rubbed for about five minutes, finally wedging his hand between my back and the sofa, but I really wasn't into him touching me right then. I'd told him that I wanted to paint like Bob Ross, just so he would get the point that I wasn't in the mood.

I sifted through the box of art supplies and felt the weight of a paint-speckled pallet in my hands.

"I guess you don't want this stuff," he said.

"Yeah, I think I changed my mind about painting."

"You don't even want to try?"

I dropped the pallette back into the box. "I want to finish watching this show, actually."

He stood there, to the side, by the coffee table, looking at me. The show cut to a commercial and I flipped through the channels.

"Whatever you want." He picked up the box and carried it toward the door.

"Where are you going?"

"I'm putting this by the curb. Someone else can take up painting."

"No, just leave it here." I had to say that, or the night would be one of him sulking, of long silences and, finally, me mustering up an apology. And whatever way it went at that point, it would conclude with sex. I might as well make it pleasant.

"What, now you want it?" he said.

"I don't know. Maybe I'm not confident yet. I might change my mind. Are you angry? Do you really want me to have it?"

"I want a talker," he said. "That's what you were when we met."

——

Weeks later, I stood at a pay phone in Penn Station with two garbage bags filled with my belongings. I was moving out. Oryn had lost his job the week before when the whole company shut down. They were commissioned to make the cap for Calvin Klein's CK One bottle, and the materials they used caused a chemical reaction with the fragrance, made it smell like dog sweat, and they had to recall a shit-load of units. They'd screwed up once before with a small shampoo manufacturer in France. It was a kids' shampoo with a ladybug cap, and the spout, which was also a spot on the ladybug, would pop off and present a choking hazard. That problem was nothing but a hundred-thousand-dollar loss—big deal—but fuck up with the big boys, and there goes your reputation. No one wants your business.

When I left Oryn's place that evening, I'd meant to go to the college and surprise James, but at Jamaica I got on a train going in the wrong direction and slept until I arrived at Penn Station.

I called James to tell him I was coming. "Come out. I want to play the game."

"Umm, can't tonight," he said.

"Fuck you can't. Come out." I checked my warped reflection in the metal plate on the phone and was reminded that I needed to bleach my roots. "Come out, come out, come out."

"Uh, well, there's this thing. There's this stuff."

"Come out."

"Who is it?" said a female voice on James's end.

"Just a friend, sweetie," he said, his voice distant. Then it came back: "Jared, I really can't."

I bought coffee at Dunkin' Donuts and sat by the escalator. A woman in heels walked quickly down, digging through her transparent purse with fingernails like tweezers, finally pulling out a Metrocard as she stepped off the last sinking step. She trotted down the corridor and around the bend, toward the subway entrance. And you can always tell the group of kids from Long Island going to a rock concert. They sat on the floor by the ticket window before heading off to the venue, laughing at their stupid jokes and posing as though everyone had their eyes on them, as though everyone wanted to be them. And then there was this couple walking in step like they fit each other, the man in his weekend denim and leather, everything scuffed in the right places; the woman's stride, draped in shining club clothes, threw back the brightness of the station. Their arms crossed each other's back, and it looked like they'd been walking that way forever. I wondered how anyone ever stayed that way— two people together unchanged—and while I watched them ride the escalator toward the exit at Madison Square Garden, waiting to see them falter, I spilled my coffee down the front of my shirt.

In the bathroom of the Long Island Rail Road waiting lounge, I changed my wet silk shirt for the college sweater I dug out from the bottom of one of the garbage bags. Paint supplies were scattered all throughout the bag. I'd thought that maybe I could sell them to some art fag once I got to the school.

When I left the bathroom, it hit me: about a hundred and twenty pounds on my back, skinny arms around my neck, and long, thin legs in big pants constricting my waist. I dropped my bags and the force of the weight pushed me forward a few steps.

"Jared!" she said. It was Shelly. She got off me and I turned to face her. I didn't know what to say. It had been the better part of a year since I'd seen her, but only a day since I'd thought about her, and when I'd thought about her she was wearing a black dress and a peacoat with pearls around her neck, her hair cascading past her shoulders. Now she wore these extra-baggy blue jeans and a white shirt with long orange sleeves and matching crewneck collar, the sleeves ending right after the elbows. Her hair was lopped off to about four inches long and purposely messy, but she was beautiful. She had an eyebrow ring. She wasn't wearing a bra.

"It's you," I said.

Shelly smiled and squealed. "Ohmigod! Jared!" She threw her arms around me. She was too loud for Shelly. "Jared! I've missed you!" She stepped back, holding on to my hands. "I saw you and your dyed hair, and I wanted to say, are you going to the concert?"

"No, I'm just passing through, actually."

"Jared!" She put her arms around me again and put her forehead against my chest. "Rub the back of my neck."

Without wondering why, I did what she asked. "Like this?"

"God, goodness yes, like that." She rested her cheek against me.

I thought of Oryn. He was probably wondering why I hadn't returned from taking out the trash.

"What are you on?" I asked Shelly.

"Oh, it's so good, Jared." She backed up and looked me up and down, still smiling. "Come. I want you to meet my friends." She pointed. "They're sitting over there." Her smile vanished. "Wait. Fuck, Rich might get bitchy if I bring you over."

Without looking toward the ticket window, I knew that Rich was in earshot. We weren't that far. Shelly was talking as though I were all the way down by the subway entrance. I turned around and sure enough there was a guy wearing pants in the same vein as Shelly's, leaning up against the newspaper recycling bin and pretending not to look at us.

"Yeah, I should probably let you go, then," I said. I wanted to sneak back into her parents' house on Long Island and spend the next day with her in her room.

"Listen," she said, her smile magically reappearing, "come by sometime."

"You still in the same dorm?"

"Yeah, so come by, like, whenever." She threw her arms around me again and kissed my cheek, then walked backward over to the booth, the whole time facing me and smiling, her Rich an insecure blur in the background.

Smoking in front of Madison Square Garden where the warm night air smelled like car exhaust and fried food, I remembered the first time I went to the city, and the air had had that same smell in pockets of heat along the sidewalk. On the way home from that trip, Sinatra's "New York, New York" came on the radio while I looked at the collage of city lights through the back window of my parents' car as we passed over a bridge, probably the Williamsburg. I remember thinking that since it was the city, "New York, New York" probably always played on the radio when you were leaving, as though the city were saying, "Farewell, and come again."

When Shelly had hugged me, I could smell her deodorant, which was the same brand she wore for as long as I'd known her. The first thing she would do when she came out of the shower was put her deodorant on, so when she hugged me at the station I had an image of her naked and wet in her bedroom, which made me think again of the bath I drew for her on that cold day in November years ago.

———

"No, really, I'm an artist. Look in my bag."

She was sitting alone at the Irish pub in Penn Station, fifty or so with sun-spotted skin and long, muscular fingers. She held a Marlboro Light like a wand. A big red kiss was embroidered on her white tank top, smack across her breasts, which moved freely under the fabric when she swayed. She was drunk—either that, or on some pills. I couldn't tell which.

"You don't look like an artist," she said.

"What does an artist look like?"

"Well, for one, they don't usually wear college sweaters. You look more like a fraternity boy." She reached her arm across the bar, held her cigarette above the ashtray, and tapped the ash off the head. The ash landed on the bar.

"But I'm a different kind of artist," I said. "I paint things to be their opposite. This way, I myself am a work of art because I'm wearing a college sweater. It's unexpected."

She looked me up and down. If she were younger, her sunken cheeks might have been exotic, but now they made her look emaciated. "Where do you show your work?"

"All over the place. I give it to my friends, and they hang them up in their apartments."

"It doesn't sound very lucrative."

"I'm not in it for the money. I paint for the love of it. I'll set up in someone's apartment, and they'll let me crash on their couch for a week, maybe feed me some, and at the end of the week they get one of the finest works of art they'll ever own."

There was a critical moment here, and I missed it while it happened, but a change came over her. In hindsight, I recall her looking off in the distance, then looking at me. She stamped her cigarette in the ashtray, her movements now suddenly languid.

"You're not super eloquent," she said. Then she leaned forward, conspiratorially. "I can tell you're raw. Your talent must be raw, too. I know, because let me tell you something." She slipped a little off her stool, caught her balance, and repositioned herself. "Artists are attracted to me—always have been, always will be. I'm a muse."

"That's the word I was going to use. You look like a muse."

"And rightly so." She smiled in that fashion-model way, where the lips flatten, as though she were about to apply liner. "Of course, you know Andy Warhol."

"The great Andy," I said. I'd heard of him.

"Yes, the great Andy. And I can say so from firsthand experience. He discovered me when I was fifteen. There are photos of me—photos Andy took. They're quite controversial and you could find them out in the world, in museums . . . private collections, I suppose."

"Really? Which museums?"

"I'm sure you'd find them at the Met. Look in the archives." She had another cigarette out. She slid the package over to me. "Controversial because"—she leaned in closer—"my genitalia are in the photos. My fifteen-year-old genitalia."

"He took pictures of your—"

"Yes. My pussy. My name, by the way, is Vanlisa."

She lived in Williamsburg. She insisted on sitting across from me on the subway, so I could study her. She arched her back, parted her legs, put a hand on each knee, and threw her head back, but her eyes, the whole time, were cast down on me. People stopped before crossing the invisible thread connecting us across the aisle.

After a few stations, she said, "Are you going to sketch me?"

"It's too bumpy," I said. "I'm taking mental notes."

Outside her apartment door, a young girl with a backpack slouched on the floor. The dim hallway was lit by tiny track bulbs lining the tops of both walls. The girl looked up to Vanlisa expectantly. A telephone rang inside the apartment.

Vanlisa stepped over the girl, unlocked her door, and bade me to enter. The two windowed walls were brick, the wood floors polished to a wet shine. In the center of the room a slab of petrified wood was the table, and the seating arrangement consisted of green fur draped over structures in all stages of becoming sofas and chairs. The windows along one wall glowed softly with Manhattan's skyline. Vanlisa left me standing there while she went to answer her phone, which was in a room behind a wall made of smoky panes of glass.

"You weren't at the station," she said into the phone. "Yes. No. Your problems. I . . . Yes, Bartos, I'm being a bitch for very good reasons."

There was no art on the walls. It looked as though she'd just moved in.

"Then come tomorrow."

When she came back into the main room, foot in front of clacking high-heeled foot, I asked her if her place was new.

"That is the wall you'll paint," she said, gesturing toward the one white wall that took up half of one side of the apartment, the other half opening to a kitchen.

"That's a big wall."

"Then you'll be a big painter," she said, walking toward one of the smaller couch-like masses. She plunked down and took her shirt off. Her breasts sagged and rounded out. She kicked off her shoes, lifted her legs, pushed her pants down, and kicked them off. She opened her legs and placed her feet apart on the sofa structure.

I couldn't make sense of her genitalia.

"Andy was fascinated, too," she said.

"Did he really take your picture?" I didn't know what else to say. It had dawned on me that I was to paint her right then—that she expected this—and I had no idea what I was doing.

"I went to his studio with my older sister. He wanted us to piss on some paintings of his."

"Why would he want you to do that?"

"Oxidation: paint reacts chemically with piss."

"Oh, yeah. Of course."

"Andy was photographing men having sex on the floor. Then he took some pictures of me."

"Pissing on his work?"

"After I pissed on his work."

I couldn't comprehend the white wall I turned to face, nor the tubes of paint I then took from my garbage bag and lined up on the floor while Vanlisa sat there watching me, waiting for my magic. All my brushes were too small. I stepped back and did some looking up and down along the wall. I stepped closer and crouched, looking up the flatness. The ceiling was so far away.

"So," I said. "So how did Andy do his work with all that distraction? Because for me, I work alone. It's sort of a private experience. I can't start if you're watching me, I mean."

She took a cigarette from the pack on the petrified table and lit it. "This is what I thought about you in the station," she said. "That you are a fraud. You are a harmless and gutless little fraud. Is that true?" She got up and walked over to me. She squeezed a tube of red paint into her hand and smeared a giant red *V* on the wall. Then, with black paint, she patted a forest of handprints over the V's crotch.

She stood back to admire her work, her hands painting her hips where she rested them. "There. Finished. Now get out of my apartment."

In the hallway, the girl with the backpack slept.

———

The last girl I went home with before I met Oryn was busy in the nose department—the kind of girl James would say was best taken from behind. The lights were out, and she started making these sounds like she was having an asthma attack. I asked her if she was okay. She started all-out bawling.

"What's wrong?" I said.

She heaved, and then her breath came out in jolts. "I don't know what I (huh!) did wrong. I don't know (huh!) why he left me."

Her crying grew louder.

With the smell of our sex in the dark, with her crying, with that loneliness between us, I could only think of Shelly holding out to me the ring I'd given her, returning it.

The girl talked into her pillow. I think she said, "I love him so much. I can't believe I love him this much."

"Don't cry, don't cry." I sat next to her. "You'll get over it, you know? It takes some time."

She cried louder into her pillow. I rubbed her naked back and she let her ass fall onto my leg. I lay next to her and continued rubbing her back, letting her soak her pillow until she settled down into a sniffle.

"We all get over these things," I said.

After a while, the girl fell asleep. I put my clothes on and left. Naked, unabashedly crying, wiping snot on the sheets in front of strangers: shit like that brought me down.

———

Shelly had said whenever—come by whenever. There was a transfer at the Jamaica station. Thirty minutes later I was on the university's commuter bus, churning toward the dormitory towers.

Shelly answered her door wearing pajamas. She let me in. Her hair was flat against her head from sleep.

I dropped my bags and hugged her.

She put her arms around me and patted my back. "Hey, what are you doing here?" She stepped away.

"You said come by whenever, right? I thought I'd come to see you."

"Yeah?" She walked over to her bed and started fixing the covers.

"It was weird seeing you last night," I said. "Penn Station of all places."

"Yeah, I was so fucked up."

"I know. You have the same comforter."

"Listen, you can sit for a while if you want to."

"Oh . . . I thought maybe we would catch up."

She put her pillow down and faced me, and then with her arms at her sides, she held her palms out to me. "I'm so sorry, Jared. I should have told you to call first."

"Well, I could wait here for you if you have to do something. We can hang out when you get back. I could use a nap anyway, you know? I don't mind, really."

"I'm going to kind of be in here," she said with this sorry look on her face. "It's my fault. I should've told you." She'd had that same look when she broke up with me, where her head was held down and tilted to the side as if she were looking at my feet but still looking at my face, though at the point farthest away from my eyes.

"You know what? I'm tired of playing games."

"Who's playing games, Jared? I'm not playing any games. I just can't break plans right now. I just can't drop—"

"Stop it, Shelly. Fucking Christ."

"I just can't—" She looked up, blinking tears off her eyelids. "What can I do, Jared? I don't know what you even want from me."

"Why the fuck do you always cry?"

"Because I don't want to hurt you."

"Then why do you? Because I don't have any money."

"I never even said that. Where do you get that?"

"Yeah, you said you were too young—"

"I said—"

"—but I got your clue. We have no car and we have no money and you don't buy me things bullshit, but you can't say it because that would make you the shallow bitch you are, you fucking—"

"I wasn't in love with you! All right?"

The room was quiet except for the sound of geese flying by and cars on the highway, noises that crept in from the outside world and seemed as far away as Shelly. A slate of clouds had blocked out the sun. She sat on her bed, looking at the floor. Once more, I slammed the door behind me.

———

On the train, I had a dream of Shelly, but she looked like Vanlisa, tall and sinewy. She was naked, facing away from me. I reached between her legs and cupped her genitalia in my hand. But she stepped away, and it came off in my grip. It was made of rubber.

The transfer was at Babylon. I stood on the station's platform and waited for the train to Floyd Harbor. I had a notebook and a pen in hand. Before I dropped out of college, I had the idea that maybe I would be good at writing. I felt like I might want to write something now—not poems—but I didn't know what to say.

A man with lips so wet I could see them shine from across the platform tried to start a conversation with some girl standing off by herself. The man looked maybe sixty, and he had a belly like a leaking sack full of mud, leaving a brown stain on the front of his shirt and pants. He held a dirty pizzeria cup. The girl saw him approaching and she turned and walked the other way with this tense expression on her face, her eyes widening.

Then he saw me.

When he talked to me, his spit hung like a loose thread between his parting lips, some of it dripping down and getting trapped in the grayish brown stubble on his face, some of it collecting in white foam in the corners of his mouth. He said, "You writing a book, buddy?" His breath smelled of whiskey.

"Brainstorming," I said. The book was empty.

He responded with a blank stare.

"I'm just putting down a few ideas."

"You want to see some ideas? Give me some paper."

I tore a page out of my notebook and gave it to him.

He forced his pizzeria cup into my hand and grabbed my pen. "What's your name?"

"Jared."

"Okay, Joey. Watch this." Then he wrote something down and handed me the paper and pen: women = cunts

He laughed loudly at this. "Do you like that?"

"Yeah, that's really good," I said, taking a step back as the breeze carried his scent to me.

"Watch this." He grabbed the pen and paper out of my hand and, using my shoulder for a writing table, he wrote: Dear Joey, be cunts.

He laughed again.

"Yeah, that's cool," I said. "Neat."

Suddenly serious, the man said, "Hey, you take care of yourself, Joey." He hugged me and leaned his head on my shoulder. His spit slid from his mouth onto my skin, and some of the drool stretched out as he pulled back, breaking off and trailing as thin as floss onto my sweater.

On the train east, I thought about what he had written, and first decided it was nonsense. He had no idea what he meant, either. What I understood was that he'd been hurt by a few women. I could tell by the pleasure he got from calling women cunts. The two times he wrote the word, this tremendous smile came across his face and he laughed as though there was nothing funnier in the world than calling women cunts—the kind of funny where you laugh from deep within your belly because you believe it's true.

But later, when I got off at Floyd Harbor in the rain, I realized something else. Unwittingly, he had told me to be a woman.

Chubba Chuck

||||||||||||||||||||||||||||||||||||||||||||||||||||||||||||||||||||||||||||

Dexter's Laboratory broke to commercial. A green lollipop floated in the foreground of a white screen. The first note on a xylophone popped and then flattened into a buzz as the proceeding notes tumbled out, the melody following a toddler taking a first step forward, swaying back, lurching forward again.

"Who wants to sucka sucka Chubba Chuck Pop?" sang a boy off screen.

A girl answered: "I wanna sucka sucka Chubba Chuck Pop."

The green lollipop turned red.

The boy sang: "Tell me, do you really want a Chubba Chuck Pop?"

The red lollipop morphed into blue, darkened to purple. "Yes, I really really want a Chubba Chuck Pop."

Then they both sang: "'Cause no one can resist a yummy yummy Chubba Chuck / Just look for the Chubba Chuck branda brand name!" And the brand name, in its trademark rainbow cursive, appeared on the white screen above the now yellow lollipop as the last notes sounded out.

The first time John heard the Chubba Chuck melody, he knew it would take up residence in a dark corner of his brain, ready to creep out in a hum in the shower, in traffic, while waiting for the ATM. The jingle worked its way into his warm-up, a little riff he'd bang out on the keys while Louis tuned his guitar, Lon checked his mic, Isaac rattled a cymbal, and Tommy walked his fingers down the neck of the bass. The melody was sticky. It had come out of John complete in a home recording one pot-infused winter afternoon. He shelved it, not knowing what to do with thirty seconds of a hook that didn't want to attach to anything resembling a full-grown song. He tried, though. The whole band tried, but finally Lon said to just leave it alone.

"It's a gem," Lon said, after devoting an hour of precious studio time to John's obsession. "It's a little masterpiece. I get you, man. Sometimes a lyric comes to me, you know, and it just lands in me, and it's a hummingbird. It's a perfect little hummingbird. It's beautiful. But you let it go. You don't cage it. Get me? Love it. Acknowledge it. And then you let it go. You get me?"

"So, you don't think we can use it somehow?" John said. "Because I think there's something to it. I think it's worth teasing it out."

Tommy, ever helpful, suggested they turn the ditty, just as it was, into a hidden track tacked onto the end of the album. Easy. Louis, though, said five rock songs followed by thirty seconds of synthesized xylophone was not really an album but a demo with thirty seconds of synthesized xylophone at the end, which was not only unprofessional, but weird. Isaac agreed with Louis, adding that they'd be lucky if anyone listening to the demo would ever make it that far into the CD. Isaac was in five bands. He knew what he was talking about. Plus, this session was costing them out of pocket, and they should stop fucking around on utter nonsense.

"He's got a point," Lon's girlfriend Alicia said. "Let it fly."

"No, yeah," John said, "I'm just throwing ideas around. Let's just shelve it for now. I agree."

Kimberly left John about a week before the commercial debuted. John came home one afternoon and saw that all Kim's things were gone: her plastic bags of modeling clay cleaned off the kitchen counter, the small plaques she'd won in community college art competitions plucked off the walls, her clothes gathered from the floor, her hairclips and bottles of nail polish collected from the top of the TV, from the windowsills, and from the bookshelf in the living room.

A vaguely citrus scent lingered in sticky rings on the bathroom sink where her toiletries had been.

John shaved. He went to open mic at the Pond Street Beanery, always on hand to accompany other musicians as they struggled or soared through three-minute sets. He went to the studio to lay down tracks for a chain of ice cream shops spreading across the eastern seaboard. They'd been impressed with Chubba Chuck. They wanted something the same, but different, for radio, and to play from the speakers of their trucks as they prowled backstreets, shopping centers, and beach parking lots for children with pocket change.

He kept a photo of Kimberly on the dresser: her hair tied back, chin up, eyes squinting, offering something between a kiss and a smirk to the camera. When she was little, a rooster she'd been chasing at a petting zoo split her upper lip. The scar from that wound, combined with a crooked front tooth, made her look as though she'd been punched in the mouth. During one of those long bedroom afternoons at the start of their relationship, John told Kimberly how much her mouth turned him on.

"Because you look so happy," he'd said, "but through all this beautiful damage." She was a community college freshman and he was doing his best to impress her. It was a line he later wrote in his song journal, thinking it would make a good lyric—*all that beautiful damage*—but one, two, three years later, when she'd bring up those early days and ask him to remind her of the line of that song he was going to write about her, he'd pretend to not remember the words. He'd come to hate them. They were stupid lyrics, no matter how he tried to sing them.

"Come on," she'd say, "you didn't forget. It's that song about my mouth."

"It's more than about that. You can't take everything literally." Her naïveté was her charm. He could teach her things, watch her discover herself—get her into the bars where he knew the staff.

And when they reached that point in their relationship where they'd talked about everything, where in their sleep, lumped on each other, they might have dreamed they were connected at the hip, or that they were spoons, or that they were an itch on the other's back, they developed the habit of recycling old conversations. Just to hear each other's voice.

"How many earrings did you used to have?" she'd say.

"You know this," he'd answer. This was in the morning, waking up.

She was half-dreaming. "But how many earrings did you used to have?"

"Five. Three in the left, two in the right."

"When did you take them out?"

"Come here," he said. But he was holding her already, the weight of her head on his chest.

"When did you take them out?"

He stroked her hair. "After high school. Come here. I have something for you."

"I was in," she said, "like, fifth grade. I was a little girl."

"Are you awake, little girl?"

"Don't be gross," she said.

The pretense of the phone call was to tell her he'd found her missing sock—a pink argyle knee-high that she'd lost months earlier, saying "John? John, come on, have you seen it? It's my favorite sock," because sometimes Kimberly was like that, clinging on to cheap objects, like when they'd walk past a street vendor who was selling sparkly plastic beads on strings and she'd gravitate toward the table mid stride, mid conversation, to pick one up to see it glint in the sunlight.

She wasn't hanging up, which would've been merciful. John couldn't hang up himself, though he had nothing more to say. He'd found the sock stuffed down between the mattress and the headboard, remembered her looking for it, and dialed her number. Maybe he'd imagined this object would transport Kimberly back to that simple moment when a sock was all she really wanted, the missing partner in a pair, the other one already pulled up her freshly shaved leg, waiting. And this simple, concrete thing—this garment—John could now provide. But it was simpler than that. No thinking involved. He found the sock, remembered her looking for it, and then called. Which was a mistake. He'd taken a meaningless, forgettable moment from her life and blown it up to excuse his contacting her.

"Say what you need to say to me," she finally said, "if that's why you called, to actually say something. Or are you really calling to tell me about a sock?"

"How can I answer that when you're making me sound stupid?"

"John, I'm not. What did I say to make you sound stupid? How am I making you sound anything? Do you realize that's why you called? About a sock?"

"I want you to come over, so we can talk."

"I can't do that. Talk here, John, on the phone."

"Why?"

"You know why."

"Why not, then?"

"Jesus, John!"

"I love you."

John felt hope in the space between this pronouncement and her answer to it, hope that lasted the length of one drawn breath, and when he was conscious of his breathing, how he was matching hers, enough time had passed to turn hope into something darker, because if his love was enough for her she would've responded already. The coating on his kitchen counter along the edges of the sink had bulked up, waterlogged, chipping in places, revealing pressboard underneath.

"Please don't do this to me," she said.

He picked at the flaking pressboard.

———

On television, a milkshake and an order of fries hung out in a swimming pool with a meatball. John had lost the plot.

Paul E held the control. He switched the television off. "Listen."

A cornfield rolled up the road to the east. Westward, a blanket of sod lay flat and trim. A red silo on the northwest edge of the property stored the grain that a farmhand, on his daily rounds, fed to the herd of bison contained in the field that shared a border with the backyard. The bison had been the deciding factor for Paul E. He said the bison would be something they had that no one else had. They were on Long Island. Not many women had seen bison before.

"What are we listening for?" John said. "I was watching that show."

"Quiet."

When Paul E was in ninth grade and excelling in Junior Varsity football, he twice brought home a girl and asked John to stay clear of their shared bedroom. At that stage, John hadn't so much as kissed a girl yet. His first kiss, in twelfth grade, had turned into a three-year relationship. His next three relationships were two years each, and his last girlfriend, Kimberly, the girl he lived with in Brooklyn before moving to the farmhouse, lasted four years. Paul E, on the other hand, didn't have relationships. He fell into infatuation with the kinds of girls who found sculpted muscles important. Likewise, it could fascinate him, for days or weeks, the way one girlfriend's face twitched as it lifted in a smile, just a little wince as though anticipating the glare of a camera flash. Paul E first thought she was always winking at him, but then he realized it was an involuntary twitch. Now though, looking back, he remembered a show he once saw about how to tell if someone's lying, and the experts talked about micro expressions, small flinches that give off when someone's not telling the truth. Not that she was lying to him. She just knew that she and Paul E were not it, and she subconsciously showed this by her twitchy smile. That was Paul E's best guess.

Anyone else might have called the end of that relationship a foregone conclusion. Paul E's relationships didn't usually last more than a month. Why would this affair be any different? The day he and John decided to make the move together, the brothers had had a boozy afternoon in the family backyard, commiserating, but John knew Paul E was just dressing up a disappointment as real heartache. It was Paul E's tendency to match himself to the situation, so even if he hadn't just split with this twitch-smile girlfriend, he'd have some other relatable tale to tell from out of his recent past. A lot of people found this relatability charming. But to John, it always felt like competition, as though in addition to everything else, they were measuring all the things that were not obvious, too, such as the weight of each other's private burdens. But they were having such a great time sharing a twelve-pack on the dock in Mastic Beach that evening that John, feeling brotherly and mischievous, pulled Paul E along as far as he could into a scheme so that by midnight,

John's vague notion of moving out of Brooklyn at the end of the month had become a concrete plan to get a bachelor pad with his brother out east for the summer. At sunrise, they waited for Handy Pantry to open so they could scan the county paper classifieds over egg sandwiches. Now here they were, weeks later, in their shared living room in a country house in Riverhead.

John reached out to Paul E for the remote control. "Come on, give it back."

"Shh! My brother is supposed to be composing a song. He's a musician. If we're quiet long enough, maybe we'll hear him play the keyboard or something."

Paul E was right. John should have been working on a song. He had a deadline for his third gig with the agency. The client wanted a selection of ideas. John had to generate them. For that, he had to get off the couch and pick up an instrument. He was supposed to be doing this musical task, and other creative work for which he now had time, while Paul E worked the overnight in the laundry room under the reception hall at the Riverhead Bath Hotel. He washed ten to fifteen loads a night and occasionally went upstairs to check the bathrooms for soap and toilet paper, see if the garbage was full. He would smoke a bowl on meal breaks at the edge of the parking lot before going back to the basement to wash another load and pump out another set of push-ups. On weekend nights, he heard from above the humming and thumping of inebriated wedding parties doing the Electric

Slide. When Paul E came home from work, John would be just a few hours from waking up, and he'd spend the day in various poses on the couch well after Paul got ready for another work night. This was all wrong. They had promised to keep the same schedule. The idea was they could then hang out more.

"Do you want to try to write a great song about car insurance?" John said.

"Let's get a six-pack," Paul E said, "and see if you have another Chubba Chuck in you."

What words could John use to express low rates for good drivers in the tristate area? He found his rhythm and sang:

Check one, check two,
Look out your rearview.
Check Point Insurance
Is always right behind you!
Check us out today,
There's no time to delay.
Oh my god, this sucks.
Paul E, go to the fridge.
Get me another beer.

By this time, Paul E had taken the tambourine off the wall:

I'm going to the fridge.
I'm getting you a beer.
Please don't have no fear,
Your beer is almost here.

For two weeks, this routine played out with variations on the same theme, until late one afternoon when Paul E came back from a run to the shopping center wearing a new black suit. John was on the couch in pajamas, doing muted finger exercises on electric guitar while watching *Between Life and Death*, a show about people in life-threatening situations caught on video.

"You bought a suit."

"I borrowed it. Cody's Department Store has a favorable return policy. It's for the wedding tonight."

"What wedding? Who's getting married?"

Paul E pulled the tie straight and brushed his hands over his sleeves. "I don't know the couple."

"Then why are you going?"

"Because I'm stuck in a routine. The same shit, every day. I sit alone in a laundry room in a basement while people party above my head. I come home to you. It's sad. I like you, but it's fucking depressing sometimes." He walked off to the kitchen. "I need some action."

"Were you invited?"

"All the people who work the reception hall are hired by the party. No one upstairs knows me. I can slip in." Paul E came back with an open beer, brushed a strand of his chin-length hair behind his ear, and looked at his reflection in the mirror by the front door, tilting his head as though offering his well-defined jawline.

On television, a segment of *Between Life and Death* ended and another began. The show relied on surveillance cameras and home video for most of its footage. After Paul E left, John witnessed, in slow motion, a gas station clerk, who had underestimated a hooded gunman, take four shots to the gut from a twenty-two pistol, the show's narrator explaining how close each bullet came to puncturing a vital organ. The show was in syndication and aired for six uninterrupted hours a day, seven days a week. John smoked and watched until the sun's glare outshone the TV. He stared at the bison through the window over the kitchen sink. Most days they looked like mounds of dirt on the far side of the field, but they had grazed right up to the electric fence at the edge of the yard today. He could see their dark eyes set in thick black fur, their dull horns. Their tails swatted at a haze of flies in the dusk. They groaned like giant empty stomachs.

John took two codeine pills left from when he had his wisdom teeth pulled. Into the late morning hours, he lay in bed, drifting in and out of sleep, feeling numb throughout his body. He had always slept with his mouth closed tight, but now it was relaxed and wide open, and he was aware of the air drying his lips whenever he woke up. He was aware of the thick stubble on his face becoming heavy with sweat. His breathing was shallow, but it seemed to fill his lungs. Awake, his sheet felt as though it was a spider's web, covered in dew and draped across his body, but it felt more like his skin while he slept. He heard a woman's voice throughout the night in thought and dream, her words barely heard, turning into a soft moan singing him back into a dream. Then she laughed so loud, so real, that it woke him up and he could still hear the laughter fading, a man's voice hushing over it.

In the morning, the farmhand's truck puttered outside. John went to take a shower but heard the water running. He went to make coffee. Paul E's suit lay scattered on the stairs. In the kitchen John found his cigarettes and lit one off the toaster. The buffalo groaned. The shower shut off, and then he heard rummaging in his room. Then he heard Paul E coming down the stairs, and then, inexplicably, saw Paul E approach the house from the far edge of the field through the kitchen window, carrying a blue cloth sack. In the living room sat a damp woman with big, dark eyes and a towel wrapped around her head, sitting cross-legged on the easy chair. She wore one of Paul E's T-shirts, and she held it down with her fists in front of her crotch.

"I'm Ashley. You must be John?"

"Yes, I am."

"Sorry if I woke you up last night. I couldn't stop laughing."

John sat on the couch across from Ashley. Her chest

pushed against the thin shirt. "No, it's okay. You're a friend of Paul E's, then?"

"Actually, I met him at the wedding last night. You should've gone."

"Oh, I wasn't feeling well."

"That's too bad," Ashley said. She shifted in the easy chair. John looked at his hands, and then stole a glance at her chest down to her crotch. She wore a small diamond ring on her left hand.

"So," she said, "what's it like having buffalo in your backyard?"

John didn't know what to say. "It's nice," he finally answered. "Really nice."

Paul E came in through the back door, carefully carrying a dozen farm eggs in his blue sack. "You guys met? Good morning. Who wants to eat?"

At breakfast, Ashley said to John, "I like your demo."

"You heard it? What demo?"

"Your band? The Letter A? Paul E played it for me last night."

"Oh, the band. Yeah, that's old stuff. You liked it?"

"That was last year," Paul E said.

"It was three years ago," John said. "Last year is when the band broke up."

"You should get back together. You guys still have the whole alphabet to get through." This was a variation of a joke Paul E made when he first heard the band name. Once he got a laugh from something, he milked it dry. *Get it? The Letter A? The other letters to get through?*

John didn't find it funny. He never liked the band name. He always felt he had to explain himself when people heard what they were called. The boring truth was that when this group of musicians answered Lon's ad and gathered for the first time in his garage, Lon suggested they arrange the first letter of each of their names into a name for the band. The only arrangement they could make any sense of spelled *Jillt.* Lon didn't like it. It sounded grungy, and the double L made the name look too death metal. They were neither grunge nor death metal. They were rock. But also, it was obvious that Lon didn't like the idea of the first letter of the keyboardist's name taking precedence. Then Lon's girlfriend suggested they name the band "The First Letter" instead. By the end of that session, they settled for the Letter A. It was just coincidence that Lon's girlfriend's name was Alicia. Letter A. Alicia. They'd somehow named the band after Lon's girlfriend. It was later that same night the new band ran into Alicia's friends at a bar. That was when John met Kimberly.

"We were together for four years," John said. "But that's over, too. I kind of moved on to other things."

"Why do you tell people that story?" Ashley said. "I think it's better to leave the name ambiguous. Ambiguity gives it intrigue. Maybe it doesn't mean 'A for Alicia.' It could mean 'A for Ashley.' Maybe it's the *Scarlet Letter* A."

That was what John disliked second-most about the

band name. People always asked if they were referencing the book by Nathaniel Hawthorne, the book everyone had to read in high school. It made the band seem like a bunch of high school lit-nerd posers.

"The E in Paul E doesn't mean anything either," John said. "It's kind of the same thing with the Letter A. It's just empty letters. Paul put the E there when we were kids because he liked the sound of it."

"See, we think the same way," Paul E said to Ashley. "And we both eat our eggs scrambled."

Ashley laughed at him.

When Paul E left to take Ashley back to the hotel, John masturbated in the shower. He imagined Ashley walking in on him. She stepped into the shower, the shirt clinging to her wet skin.

Later that morning, John and Paul E smoked a bowl. Then, at the back edge of the cornfield, they sat on a defunct tractor and smoked a joint. They opened whiskey in the evening and drank from the bottle while jamming with John's instruments. They had the keyboard on a steady beat while John played guitar and Paul E banged the tambourine.

John sang:

I'm a tractor to her
I want to plow her field.
I'm a tractor to her,

I want to plant my seed,
I'm a tractor to her
But no, no, no,
No, no, no, no,
She's not attracted to me.

It was in the seventh chorus of this song that John, with a joint in the corner of his mouth, said, "Hey, hey. Wait. I gotta lay down." He fell to the floor.

Paul E put the tambourine down. He looked at John. "John?"

John struggled getting up, fumbling with the guitar strapped over his shoulder. He took a few steps back, touched the wall to steady himself, then took a few steps forward. He looked at Paul E. "Paul E, I need to sit." John fell to the floor again.

Paul E put a pillow under his brother's head and covered him with a blanket.

The first segment of the show was about a girl trapped inside her white convertible. She tried to pass a car by going into the left lane and hit a blue Toyota Celica head on. The guy in the Toyota walked away from the accident. There was a graduation party going on at the house opposite where the accident happened, and the guy working the camcorder got the whole ordeal on film.

Paul E came into the living room. He had his suit on. He was going to work. Another wedding.

"Tie is on the coat rack," John said.

"Thanks. How's your head feeling?"

"What happened last night?"

"You got really fucked up."

"No, I mean after that."

"Well, you fell down," Paul E said, walking back to the couch with the tie. "Then you got up and fell down again." Paul sat on the couch and looped the tie around his neck. "Then I went out."

"Where'd you go?"

"Actually, it's pretty funny what happened."

"My god!" they heard from the television. On the screen, the convertible lay on its side, bent up into an arch, driver side down. The girl was hanging from the car, torso and arms stretched out in the space between the dent in the car and the ground, as if reaching for a loose bit of gravel. But she wasn't moving. The only thing on the screen that moved was her brown hair, blowing gently against her forearms in a slight breeze.

"Holy shit," Paul E said. "That girl is dead."

"They never show dead people on this show. So, what happened last night?"

Paul still had his eyes on the screen. "I picked up a hooker."

"Shut up."

"No. Riverhead. Right by the traffic circle. She was standing on the corner. I drove up, and she got in."

"How did you know she was a hooker?"

"Young girl, butt-load of makeup, black miniskirt, two in the morning. She wasn't waiting for a school bus."

"In Riverhead?"

"Why not? There's hookers everywhere." Paul E looped his tie.

"What did she look like?"

"Well, she was kind of like that doped-up chick from Fleetwood Mac."

"Stevie Nicks?"

"Yeah, but different. She was younger and better-looking. So, she gets in and I start driving, and right away she asks if I'm a cop. I say, 'No.' Then she says, 'So you want a blow job?' I was like, 'Whoa, slow down. Talk to me. Let's get to know each other. What's your name?' She says, 'Rosie. My name is Rosie.' Then—"

"That's not her real name. Hookers never give their real name."

"Let me finish. All right, so we were driving, and she started getting scared because I was asking her stuff, like what she likes to do and where she went to school, and she said . . . How did she say it? Something like, 'Why you all proper and shit?' and I said, 'Look, I'm not going to treat you that way.' Then she was all fidgety, tapping her nails on the window, stuff like that. Now I'm driving down our street, almost at the house, so I slow down, and she said,

'No, I don't like this.' She opened the door and jumped right the fuck out."

"Shit. Was she all right?"

"Yeah, she ran back toward town. I've never seen anyone run in heels like that."

"What did you do?"

"I said, 'Rosie! Come back! We can do the blow job thing if you want!'"

John chuckled, unsure if this was just one of Paul E's dumb jokes.

"I really didn't say that to her, but that would've been funny, huh?"

"Wow. She ran all the way back?"

"I guess. Unless she got picked up." Paul E straightened his tie. "Listen, I'm going. Take care of that headache."

"Wait," John said, "I'll go with you. I'll need the car."

"You have to go somewhere?"

"No, I just need to get out a little. Get a haircut. I've been in this house too long. I can pick you up later."

On the television, paramedics pulled the girl from the car and laid her out on a stretcher, covering her face.

"That's fucked up," Paul E said.

The focus was on the girl's covered face, her wrecked car a blur in the background. It reminded John of a sculpture he and Kimberly saw in a park once. It was made from prefabricated metals welded together, and it looked like nothing. Kimberly had said, in her naïve, freshman art student way, that it could represent love because no one could agree what that was either. John thought that what he saw on the screen was a better representation of love. Two random people collide. Someone gets hurt.

"Yeah," John said, "I thought they didn't show any deaths."

Coming back from dropping Paul E off, John got a haircut and a shave. At home, he showered and flossed. He ironed a pair of khakis. He figured she would be there around midnight. That would give him three hours before he had to pick up Paul E.

He left the house a little after twelve, drove down Roanoke Avenue, past the cornfields, past the North Quarter Horse Stable. It was a four-mile drive to the traffic circle. He wondered what corner she would be on. Paul E never said. The 7-Eleven? The hospital?

She was standing in front of the closed-down Pizza Hut, looking just the way Paul E had described, at least from behind. Since she was facing the opposite way, she could not have seen John pull up. John wished she had. Her hair was long and black. Her arms were crossed, and she was smoking. Her skirt was almost short enough to be a very wide belt. If she bent over or even walked too fast, anyone watching would get flashed.

He pulled up to her so all he could see was her waist and chest through the passenger window.

"Uh-uh," she said. "No. I'm not getting in that car with you."

John leaned over, so they could see each other's face.

"Oh," she said. "You got the same car as this weirdo." She opened the door and got in. "Are you a cop?"

"No."

She looked him up and down. "You want a blow job?"

"How much?"

"Twenty. Thirty if you want me to do the whole thing. To finish." She was young, maybe eighteen. Her eyebrows were shaped, her lips painted red, black eyeliner, but that was all. She wasn't painted like a clown, the way Paul E made it seem. She smelled like vanilla.

"That's good," John said. "I'll do that."

"Do what? Which one?"

"The thirty."

"Where's the money?"

John handed her thirty dollars from his wallet. She stuffed it down her tank top, between her breasts, and leaned across the seat for John's zipper.

John grabbed her hand. "Right here? We can go to a motel or something. I mean, if you want."

"If you're paying. Go up to the Bath."

"Is there another hotel?"

"Yeah, the Riverhead. Down 25 a few miles, but you have to bring me back."

He let go of her hand and let his foot off the brake.

They went down Route 25 in silence, John and his hooker. He wondered if it was right to think of her that way. Hooker. What did she prefer? Ho? Whore? Prostitute? Rosie? What could he say to her? Nothing. Then what? She was sitting still, her eyes on the road. Should he ask her how she was doing?

"I was wondering what your name is," he said.

She continued watching the road. "Donna. My name is Donna."

"I'm John."

"It's about six more miles."

"Okay."

And it was silent again. John tapped the steering wheel. The hooker rested her head against the window. She ran her left hand through her hair once then placed it back on her lap. John thought about turning the radio on, but now he couldn't make his hand reach out anywhere near her. He wondered again if there was anything that he could say to her, something that she hadn't been asked a million times. He wondered where she sat to pluck her eyebrows, what the perfume she wore was called. Anything to break the silence. Seemingly perpetual silence: it made him feel like he was waiting and waiting and waiting.

He mumbled, "Who wants to sucka sucka Chubba Chuck pop?"

She looked at him with surprise.

"Sorry," he said.

She turned her head back against the window. She glanced at John. Twenty seconds passed as she continued to watch the road, the green light of an intersection, a dealership full of shiny new cars.

John looked at her and saw that her lips were pursed.

She glanced at John and let out a laugh. Self-consciously, she sang, "I wanna wanna sucka Chubba Chuck pop."

John smiled. He looked at her and said, "Tell me, do you really want a Chubba Chuck pop?" He darted his eyes between the hooker and the road.

"Yes, I really really want a Chubba Chuck pop."

They both sang louder, "'Cause no one can resist a yummy yummy Chubba Chuck! / Just look for the Chubba Chuck branda brand name!"

She laughed so hard that she had to hold her waist. She snorted like a piglet. "Holy shit! That's so funny you sang that! That's my blow job song!"

"Your what? Your blow job song?"

She slapped her hand down on John's knee and took a moment to catch her breath a little, her head back and her mouth a toothy, open smile. "You know, like when I'm going down on a guy and I don't want to think about it? It makes me laugh inside."

"That's funny. I wrote that song."

"You fucking liar!" she said in playful disbelief.

John looked over to her. "No, really. That's what I do."

"You really wrote that?"

"Seriously."

"That's such a blow job song!"

John smiled even bigger. "I never thought of it that way. I guess that's the only way I'll know it now."

The motel came up on the left. John pulled onto the shoulder and turned into the parking lot. He felt her hand still resting on his knee. He found a parking space and turned the car off. He looked at her.

She was looking at her hand on his leg. "My name is Amber," she said. "Amber's my real name."

"I'm John."

"Yeah, I know. You told me."

In the motel room, the hooker sucked John's penis for the thirty dollars he had given her. He sat on the edge of the bed with his pants down and she knelt on the floor. When she took him into her mouth he held her head behind her ear as if guiding her in the right direction, as if she were spoon-feeding. Then, with sudden force, John pushed himself deeper in. She gagged.

"I'm coming, Amber," John said under his breath. "I'm coming. I'm coming."

It had taken fifteen minutes from the time they walked into the room to make John have an orgasm. She went into the bathroom to wash up. When she came out, John was still stretched out on the bed with his feet on the floor and his pants around his shins.

"You said you would drive me back when we're finished."

"Yeah." He pulled his pants up and buckled his belt while she walked over to the door. He followed her out to the car, watching her walk to the passenger side with her arms crossed in front of her. She waited for him to unlock the door. He was to drop her at the traffic circle.

Battery

||||||||||||||||||||||||||||||||||||||||

The properly inhaled cigarette smoke was doing something bristly behind my eyes. Jay-Jay had capped his head in a red bandana so that his hair stuck out like wings over his ears. He slouched against his dresser with his thumbs hooked in the pockets of his jeans, telling me about a yellow Caprice Classic for sale on the street behind Pathmark. He said he'd own that car one day.

"I'll drive to anywhere I want. I'll be fucking gone. Can you see it?"

That was when our neighborhood blacked out. I couldn't see anything.

"I'll get a flashlight," Jay-Jay said. "Hold this."

I reached into the darkness.

He dropped his dick in my hand and laughed.

The next day we shared a forty of Hurricane in the woods behind Handy Pantry, in a clearing beyond a small mountain of busted sidewalk. Jay-Jay did most of his thinking there. He did most of his thinking out loud. But on the day after the blackout, Jay-Jay didn't share his thoughts. He just stared at the trees as he did pull-ups from a low branch hanging over the clearing. It was the day Theresa was being released from juvie hall.

"Where are you supposed to meet her?" I said, gesturing with the forty as though shifting a jet's throttle, the way I'd seen Jay-Jay hold the bottle and talk.

He dropped from the branch, unzipped his pants. "Nowhere." He peed on a broken bottle. "We'll just find each other."

There was a rumor that Theresa was once pregnant by a motorcycle guy. One time at this house party, Theresa disappeared to a bedroom where I was hiding from this guy who had hooked and yanked my crotch with the handle of an old-lady cane, just for laughs. Theresa said she wanted to try on some of the clothes. She slipped into a blue gown and checked herself out in the mirror. The dress needed to be zipped up the back. She was also having trouble clasping the necklace she'd found in the jewelry box. As I helped her out, she told me that whenever she was alone with a guy she would end up fucking him. I left her there in the room.

———

We found Theresa on the pink patio of John's Pizzeria on Neighborhood Road, sitting at one of the plastic tables with her juvie friend Alice.

Jay-Jay introduced me to Alice as Whipping Boy.

"You're my boyfriend today," Alice said to me. Her fingernails were painted black.

"I don't mind," I said. "You're beautiful." I was brave enough to say this because I was drunk.

What a hot day. Jay-Jay squeezed Theresa and they walked ahead, not really on the way to anywhere. The sidewalks were ours. Most people just drove by, stopping only to run into Handy Pantry or the smoke shop. A bungalow we passed had been turned into what looked like a bait store. A seascape was painted on the display window.

"Why do they call you Whipping Boy?" Alice said.

"Because I'm younger than him, I guess. I'm smaller."

"I like your size."

We were soon in a new house on the creek where no one lived. Alice and I looked through the glass doors at some floating ducks near the cattails. Jay-Jay took Theresa to the empty bedroom.

"Kiss me," Alice said.

I hadn't thought about kissing her. Was she really beautiful? Her hair was mostly blond except by her scalp, where the roots were brown. She had wide cheeks that bunched under her eyes when she smiled. Her arms looked good for giving headlocks. We kissed, and we kept kissing for a long time, her mouth a dark room I felt my way around. We smoked more of her cigarettes, and she showed me how she'd painted her nails by painting mine.

The next morning, my mother trapped me for family time. Brian was back with a promise to stick around and help with rent, the reasons behind the celebration of eggs and sausages. We washed breakfast down with real orange juice that had bits of orange floating in it. Mom turned up the radio and then opened the windows. She washed the dishes. The ashtrays gleamed. I rinsed the empties. It was not enough to be worth cashing in yet, but I still had money from the last empties.

Brian had spread the classifieds out. He said he only needed the right job to get walking a straight line. He said his problem was he had no connections.

"What about from one of your last jobs?" my mom said. "Can't you get a reference?"

"The problem's everything's so goddamn far from here."

"You can take the bus," Mom said. "And there's a bike in the basement. The last people left it there. You can ride it to catch the bus on Montauk Highway."

"That's my spare bike," I said. "I claimed that Huffy when we moved here."

"I'm sure you can let Brian use that one," my mom said. "Don't be selfish. You don't even ride your first bike. Why do you need two?"

"I need it for parts."

And then Brian said, "Jeez, are you wearing nail polish?"

"Since when do you fix bikes?" Mom asked.

"It's *black* nail polish," I said. "So what?"

"So why are you wearing nail polish?"

"Everyone wears black nail polish. You used to wear earrings, Brian. Remember?"

"I wore one in my left ear, but then I grew up."

"When did that happen? I must have missed that."

"I liked your earring," my mom said.

"I have to go," I said. "People are waiting for me."

"You got a beauty appointment?" Brian said.

"Go fuck yourself."

Then Mom said she wished I wouldn't curse.

I told her I wished she wouldn't let a fucking loser live in our house.

Jay-Jay lived over on Woodside Road. His front door was unlocked. His mother snoozed on the couch. His father's urn watched over from atop the television. How did his father die? My father died when he was stabbed for eleven dollars and thirteen cents, but that was before I was born, and it happened in another town where my mother used to live, and she didn't really know my father that well, anyway. The story was told to my mother months after the fact by secondhand people. The exact details were questionable. The point was, he wasn't killed for much. Also, I would never know him. But that's life. Some things remain a mystery. Like why was there a stack of microwave boxes at the bottom of the basement stairs?

"What the fuck are you doing?" Jay-Jay said. Theresa lay in bed next to him. In the basement, you wouldn't know the sun had been baking the streets for hours already.

"I have a present," I said. "It's outside."

Jay-Jay's shady yard was too bright for him, but then he lit a cigarette and relaxed. He'd wrapped his brown sheet around himself and it made him appear like an owl, wisely pacing around the bikes, widening his eyes and inspecting the frames and smoking and scratching his head.

"Who did you steal these from?" Jay-Jay said.

"They're mine," I said. "Ours."

"You woke me up for this?"

"We can go farther now," I said, "instead of walking the same blocks."

A motorcycle roared past the tangle of vines that hid Jay-Jay's house from the neighbors, sweeping away the summer feel and leaving us with the smell of gas station.

Jay-Jay said, "I always thought I was dreaming that motorcycle."

The birds living in the vine fence started getting their chirps back.

"Do you want to try these bikes?"

"I want to sleep," he said.

———

My bike's chain skipped, and his bike had no brakes and a crooked wheel. That night we rode them to the 7-Eleven, south on William Floyd Parkway, to find someone to buy us beer with my empties money. The only help we could find in the parking lot was a guy who said, "Sure," but instead of getting us beer, he bought us hot dogs as a joke. Then he gave us four pieces of acid. I'd never taken acid before.

At the empty house by the creek, Alice said the acid was showing her how love worked by drawing pictures in her mind. She saw the letters that spelled the word *love* floating from one person's mouth and finding another person's ear, like the way she was whispering in my ear while she knelt on the floor. I lay with my face inside the tent of her two-tone hair.

"The letters keep changing," she said. "The people of my mind are flat."

Jay-Jay had left to pee a long time ago, and Theresa was sitting on my chest and asking if Jay-Jay was serious about her.

"Serious how?" I asked.

"She means in love," Alice said. "Is he in love with her?"

"I don't understand," I said. It was too much pressure.

"I just explained what love is," Alice said. "Just now."

"Am I wasting my time?" Theresa said.

"We would know how he felt if he said something," I said. "Where is he?"

Then a duck quacked, and outside the sliding glass door, Jay-Jay stood naked in the cattails, holding a duck in both hands down between his knees. He was the second-brightest thing outside, next to the white duck, and the whole scene felt like it had happened before, like I'd seen this part in a movie about my life. He launched the duck into the night. The wings clapped ever higher.

Jay-Jay eventually looked down from the empty sky and opened the sliding glass door.

"How do you feel about me?" Theresa said.

Jay-Jay did not speak, just scooped up Theresa, who happily yelped, and carried her into the bedroom.

"How do you feel about me?" Alice said.

I could see she wanted me to touch her.

Birds sang the aches of my joints in the morning. Brian was in the living room, with empties huddled around his chair.

"You're home late," he said.

"It's early," I said. I wanted something to weigh my stomach down, but there was only grease in the leftover sausage container and toast from the day before. My mother hadn't planned her new life with Brian beyond that breakfast.

"The bike's gone," he said, "so how could I get to an interview?" A line of blood had dried on his neck.

My knuckles chirped.

"I found this earring because Mom wanted me to have one. She wouldn't shut up about the earring. I put the earring in my ear. That's the result of the whole thing. I hope everyone is amused." He held his hair back to show the bloody pearl against his earlobe. He had a look like he might jump up to smack me, but it was a bluff.

Down the hall in her room, my mother slept on her bed, cuddling the junk drawer she'd pulled from her dresser. She'd been looking through her matchbooks and skinny jewelry from old times. The good old days, she'd say. Something blue and purple had happened to her cheek, below one eye. The chirping birds had become police sirens, sketching out a curve onto Neighborhood Road by the sound of it.

"I'm amused," Brian said from the kitchen. "I'm goddamn fucking amused."

When I woke later and checked in on Mom, she was still sleeping, or sleeping again, the junk drawer now on the floor and Brian in its place under her arm.

Jay-Jay squatted in his front yard, cleaning the crud off a set of ball bearings with a rag. On a flattened cardboard box, he had separated and arranged the bike I'd given him into frame, handlebars, pedals, chain, tires, rims, and crank.

"I'm fixing this," he said.

"I'm gonna have sex with Alice," I said.

"Leave your bike here. I'll fix the chain." Then he gave me condoms and showed me how to put one on, using a broomstick he found in the basement for the dick. I watched him put his bike back together. He started working on mine when Alice and her dad showed up in his car to take me away.

"You kids need anything?" her dad said as we took off.

Alice said, "Can you buy us forties?"

He'd been out of jail for almost a year. The methadone made him look like he'd just awoken from a great nap. He parked in front of his split-level and yawned. They lived upstairs.

"I'm trying to be a good dad," he said in Alice's bedroom.

I rocked in her white rocking chair. The last sips of Hurricane swished in the bottle.

Alice cuddled up on her bed with her plush bear, plush zebra, and giant plush tropical bird. "You're a great man, Daddy," she said.

"I put this room together just for her. I bought those blankets and I found that mirror. I fixed that dresser. All those knobs on the drawers are new."

He insisted we all sleep in the king-size bed that took up most of his room. He didn't want to leave us unsupervised.

Alice took the middle of the bed. Her dad took the outside. I got the wall. There was a smell of mouthwash. Under the blankets, Alice cupped my penis through my jeans.

"This is kind of weird," I whispered. "Your father's sleeping, right there."

With each breath, his chest crackled unevenly but rhythmically, like the crank on a jack-in-the-box. He was like my father had been, I imagined—the kind of man who might die over small change.

"He's on his pills," she said. "He won't wake up."

"I don't know."

She cuddled up to me, kissed my neck, and wedged her hand between my legs. We fell into an uneasy sleep.

The refrigerator was the color of a treasure map. Alice cooked eggs and some bacon she found. It was noon and her father had left for the clinic before we awoke.

After breakfast, we made out in the kitchen doorway, and Alice took her shirt off. We rubbed against each other on her bed for a while. She pushed her breasts against me and reached into my pants. I slid away from her grasp. She said she wanted my cock.

She must have known I was a virgin as I didn't take my cock out, and I guess knowing that I was a virgin, and sensitive, was why she didn't directly point out that our grinding was going nowhere. Instead she smiled and said, "I got this idea. Put panties on. I want to see you in my underwear." She went to her top drawer and pulled out a thong. "Try these."

"I don't know."

"Please?"

"Why?"

"I want to see."

"I don't know," I said, and took the panties from her. Then I said I needed to go to the bathroom.

"Come back with the underwear on."

The bathroom was like a narrow hallway. Specks of white toothpaste spattered the faucet. I was getting hard trying to stuff myself into the underwear when the phone rang. I heard Alice pick it up in the kitchen.

"How was I supposed to know?" she said. "It's not your grass, either. What was I supposed to do with it?"

I assumed the conversation was about drugs. I thought she was talking to her father. I put my pants back on and went to the kitchen.

"That was the man downstairs," Alice said. "He says we burned a spot on the lawn. What are you supposed to do with hot bacon grease anyway?" She wasn't wearing pants anymore. Her panties were like mine, but hers were blue with tiny purple flowers along the edges. The front patch of fabric formed a curved triangle.

My panties pinched my balls into saddlebags. "What's your father going to say?"

"About what?"

"The grass."

"Are you wearing them?"

"Yeah."

"Let me see." And then she was kissing me, opening my pants and grabbing my sagging dick, pulling at it, while with her other hand she wedged the string of my panties up my butt. She nibbled my bottom lip.

I squeezed her breasts. I touched her hip. The kitchen smelled like bacon. I found a bump on her shoulder and picked at it a little, but then I grabbed her breasts again.

"What's the matter?" she said.

"I don't know. I have a strange feeling. I can't concentrate."

"Do you want to see my father's magazines?"

They were behind a stack of towels in the hall closet. She brought one to the bedroom. She had looked at the magazine before and opened it to a picture for me to look at. The man aimed his penis at the girl's open mouth. She looked up at the man thankfully. Then there were pictures of them having sex in ways that showed all the details anyone would want to see. When I was hard enough from looking, Alice got into position on the bed. I took a condom from my bag and rolled it on the way Jay-Jay had shown me. Then I turned the light off and got in bed on top of her.

"I'm ready," she said.

I began to soften before I could enter her, and when I pushed against her my penis just squirmed around between her thighs.

"Think of the pictures," Alice said. She had her father's thin lips. I wondered if her mother had the same cheeks. I wondered what our baby would look like. All this wondering happened while I envisioned Jay-Jay, with his expert hands, showing me how to squeeze the breast and grab the hip, and entering Alice vanished under these thoughts as though I'd always been inside of her.

"You did it, though, yeah?" Jay-Jay shouted.

"Then her father came home, so we stopped," I shouted back.

Jay-Jay wanted details.

I wanted to know how he traded the Huffys for a motor-bike in the twenty-four hours I'd been gone.

The engine puttered and coughed. He disconnected the car battery that he'd used to do a jump-start.

"So now we have a motorcycle," I said.

"No," Jay-Jay said, straddling the seat, stroking the side. "Theresa doesn't like it."

I remembered the story about the motorcycle man.

"Get on," Jay-Jay said.

The town was asphalt and traffic light. I wished for a helmet when he blew through backstreet stop signs, for kneepads when we took the long curve of Riviera Drive along the bay. The thong rode up on me. We took a dirt trail through Mastic to North Floyd Harbor. When we arrived at Pathmark, I was glad to be alive. Jay-Jay told me to wait in the parking lot, and he took off again.

Between me and the shopping carts, a woman wearing headphones sang in a low mumble. She'd been in that parking lot since before we moved to that town. When my mother and I came to Pathmark to buy our first groceries, I had waited outside and watched the lady sing. People called her the Pathmark lady. If you wanted an easy way to make fun of someone, you'd just say she was their mom. She wore a few different dresses at once and used rubber bands for bracelets. When she hit the low notes, she'd tuck her chin into her neck. For the high notes, she lifted her head to the sky and bared her teeth like she was trying to bite a grape off a vine.

Now she dropped her tape player and the battery case popped open. The case was empty. There was no sound. She was making it up, pretending to be in sync with music that wasn't there. She picked the player up and reattached the battery case door. She saw that I saw and scowled at me as though I were accusing her, like why couldn't I let her pretend to hear music that wasn't there?

Right then, Jay-Jay came back in the yellow Caprice Classic. Theresa sat next to him. I got in the backseat, with Alice.

"Where to, kids?" Jay-Jay asked in the rearview mirror. Montauk Highway's traffic hummed like a vacuum. Clouds were gathering from the northeast.

"How did you get this car?" I said.

"I traded the motorcycle." Jay-Jay pulled a Kool from a soft pack with his teeth.

An old bumper sticker on the dashboard said WHERE'S DA HARBOR?

Theresa lit Jay-Jay's cigarette with a tall purple lighter.

A strand of Alice's hair tickled my lip. We were that close. She nodded toward the parking lot lady. "I wonder what song she's singing. She's always singing."

Jay-Jay shifted into drive, and the car inched forward.

"She's probably singing a love song," I said. "One from the good old days."

Holiday

IIIIIIIIIIIIIIIIIIIIIIIIIIIIIIIIIIIIIIIIIIIIII

The day after the layoff, instead of going to the unemployment office, they sunbathed in Keith's yard under an energy-sapping sky. Keith's rented Kingman ranch house was one of a dozen on a narrow street alongside the railroad near the Floyd Harbor station. His chickens, when they weren't shitting in the driveway, liked to peck the gravel near the tracks on the other side of the fence. When the train came through they'd scratch their way back over, clawing a broken board here, launching off a paint bucket there, their wings beating like caught fish. Chickens can't fly, but Keith's gave it their best. Once atop the fence, the ambitious girls floated down, landed feetfirst, and dashed across the yard. The careless ones fell on their chests, and they'd go tripping along the ground before they got their footing. They'd hide in the shade under the boat on the trailer that was permanently parked in the driveway.

"'Green Pastures,'" Keith offered. He soaked in a plastic kiddie pool, a foam cooler full of iced beer at his side. He gripped a can in his meaty hand.

"'Scenic Landscaping,'" Dan said. "'Keith and Dan Landscaping.' 'Big Fat Goddamn Green Thumb.'" There was a van for sale down the block. Dan had the number on a napkin in his pocket. He'd spread a beach towel with an airbrushed wind sail on it and planted himself in a shallow, grassy depression where the chickens tended not to shit. The depression was roughly the size of a twin bed, about as deep as a crock pot. He sipped his beer. The radio played "Hotel California" for the second time that afternoon. A white feather rolled along the ground by his feet. "How many chickens you have, do you think?"

"Two dozen," Keith said, "give or take." His belly stuck out from the water's surface, and he flicked his finger at the pool in his navel.

"Why so many?" Dan asked.

"Well," Keith started, but then the 2:10 train came chugging down the tracks with its whistle wailing. Dan couldn't hear what Keith said. Instead of asking him to speak up, Dan just watched the chickens flop and flutter over the fence and then scramble down the dirt driveway, all the way to the end, where some pressed their calico chests against the chain-link separating the yard from the street, others cluttered and milled around one another, jerking their heads with suspicion, chattering their chicken talk, the train's roar now a memory just as loud as the moment it passed, like something stupid blurted out that hangs around in your mind for a while, beating you down, but then Dan slurped his can empty and the radio lifted him with the last chorus.

The Eagles sang, "Such a lovely place (such a lovely place)."

Keith swished in his sparkling lagoon.

Dan closed the red impression of the sky behind his eyelids and drifted, like a napkin on a breeze, to where a flock of chickens soared above the power lines.

The Luz

||||||||||||||||||||||||||||||||||||||||

In March, Mr. Luzzi packed his grammar posters. He checked and signed the classroom inventory form in April. In May, he wrote predictive blurbs for report cards that were due in June, and then he watched the clock as his sophomores bent over timed essays on *Of Mice and Men*.

At graduation, Luzzi hoped to sneak off the field before the close of the ceremony, but Lisa Baker had Frank Luzzi in her sights from "Pomp and Circumstance." He could feel her like a ghost, three rows back to his left. By the third speech, Luzzi's neck hurt from the tension. He got an idea. He patted himself down and reached inside his suit, taking a folded paper from the inside pocket. He consulted the paper as he stood, running a finger over the lines. Then he walked down the bleacher stairs. The folded paper was the beginning of a story Luzzi had started writing in December, during a Friday meeting, but to anyone watching him it would appear Luzzi was preparing to deliver a speech of his own. Stepping off the bleachers, he walked through the loose crowd of mothers of crying babies and restless toddlers on the sidelines, around the outer edge of the track field, behind the graduation stage, along the gymnasium, past the tennis courts, around the Dumpsters, behind the cafeteria. At the front gate, a cluster of young male relatives of the graduates smoked, chatted, paced, and spit. They were on the campus side of the fence, testing the limits of the new smoking ban.

"The Luz," one of the scruffy men said as Mr. Luzzi passed through to the other side. "Good summer, Luz."

"You, too," Luzzi said, turning back to address the general crowd with a wave of his car keys. He didn't know who had wished him a good summer. A former student from five years or a decade ago. These guys used to smoke right outside the lobby doors. Behind the school gate, dressed in those ill-fitting, emergency-only suits, they looked like they were awaiting court appearances. Some of them probably were.

Lisa Baker's route to the parking lot had been through the building. She waited by Mr. Luzzi's Toyota. She held a bouquet of daisies.

"Lisa," Luzzi said. "You'll miss graduation."

"I can't let you leave without thanking you. You really believed in Roland. You're the reason he's getting that diploma." She presented the flowers.

"No, no," Luzzi said, accepting the bouquet as though a stranger had just invited him to hold her baby. "It was all Roland. Besides, he had you supporting him at home."

"You're too modest. I'm just glad he'll always have those reports you wrote. It only takes a few good words. You saw that. You really did. Give me a hug." She held Luzzi in an embrace. When Luzzi put his arms around her shoulders, she squeezed tighter.

"Always the feeler," Mr. Luzzi said.

"Shut up and hug me back. Doofus."

Mr. Luzzi returned the embrace. A small plane flew overhead, probably hired by one of the graduation committees of the wealthier North Shore schools, probably trailing a sign congratulating the seniors, and for a moment, giving in to the warm bulk of Lisa's bosom, an earlier part of Mr. Luzzi's life tapped him on the shoulder—brimming glass of beer in hand, he was sitting on a barstool where he had a view of the private planes taking off and landing at Brookhaven Calabro Airport. His divorce was final, his stillborn daughter buried out in Riverhead, his tenure in the district a few years away. Any minute, a younger Lisa Baker would walk through the door, a girlfriend at each elbow. One of the girlfriends was the Lamaze instructor from the class Mr. Luzzi and Lisa Baker had taken at Saint Jude's Church with their respective spouses. He didn't know the other woman. They took a corner table: a support group for Lisa Baker, Luzzi had concluded, a guess buoyed by the rumor that Mr. Baker had followed his job to California a year earlier, never sending back for Lisa and the baby. Luzzi put the writing pad away and turned on his stool for a better view. Lisa had noticed.

"You're going to miss the graduation," Luzzi said into the bouquet.

"They're still doing speeches."

Principal Feeney was giving another long-winded introduction to another honored member of the Floyd community who would inevitably deliver a tract of advice to the graduates much like they'd been given in the previous speech. It was the same every year. Feeney's amplified voice filled the sky above the parking lot like a cloud of echoes.

Lisa broke the embrace and pinched Luzzi's graying goatee. "We need to catch up. I get stories about you from Roland, but I'd like to hear directly from you, too. Come around sometime."

"I will."

Did Lisa know the cancer had come back and would take her within two months? That this was the last time she and Frank Luzzi would see each other?

If Mr. Luzzi had to give Lisa Baker a report on Roland now, three years post-graduation, he would say that Roland is a student of life, always curious to see what goodies have been stored atop the refrigerator of adulthood, but since he hasn't grown enough to see for himself, he relies on imagination, which leads him to skew reality in novel ways.

Roland's face fills the screen, and he peers as though into a magnifying glass, scrutinizing the viewer. The shot widens, and a background of stained glass washes out with sunlight. A halo rings the silhouette of Roland's buzz-cut head. The chatter of a congregation cedes to a church organ and the screen whitens. Then the film turns blue and silent. Then it features the back of a woman's head. She wears a veil. There stands an inaudible preacher.

The shot drifts to show the crown of the groom's head, bottom right on the screen, and Jesus's feet nailed to the cross, farther back, top left. Then it pans down, lingering on a tribal sun tattoo on the back of a bridesmaid's neck in the front pew. This part is narrated by Roland, whispering into the built-in mic, *That's not the method I use*, and by another man who insists in hushed tones that, if a cameraman plans on taking steady shots, he should attach the camera to a tripod instead of holding it against his cheek.

That's not the method I use.

I'm just trying to help you, the man grumbles.

To which Roland replies, *That's not the method I use. I'm telling you, that's not the method I use.*

"What are we watching?" Mr. Luzzi says. His pale legs stick to the black leather couch. The morning sun bakes the living room. He had been doing stretches, almost ready for a run, when Roland showed up.

Roland is standing, remote in hand. He's grown half a

foot since Luzzi saw him last. "That talking guy is the uncle of the bride. He wanted to control me."

"That's not what I meant, Roland. What's this film about? I can't handle the suspense anymore."

"Just tell me what you think, Mr. Luzzi. Not now. I'll say when."

It's not clear how much Roland knows about the past Mr. Luzzi shared with the boy's mother, for whatever that past is worth. It's enough of a past that, for a time, people who didn't know the facts had assumed Frank Luzzi was the father of baby Roland. There were beach days, Sunday brunches, theater tickets, a long weekend in Manhattan. Before the foreclosure on the Baker house, there were enough late-night returns to wake the babysitter and drive her home to call it a routine. Six months can feel like a lifetime. Mr. Luzzi wonders if that time left an imprint on the child, too, or if boys without fathers simply take to any next available candidate for Dad—the mailman, store clerk, corner drunk, teacher. Did Roland approach them all with the same affability?

"Good morning, Mr. Luzzi," Roland had said the first day of grade ten. Luzzi didn't recognize the boy at first. It had been that long. "What are we learning in English today?"

"Rolly's in this class?" said the next boy entering the room. "Oh, great."

"How long is this video, Roland?"

"On this tape?"

The scene jerks around as though an earthquake had struck. Director Roland had decided to attach the camera to the tripod after all, but while continuing to film. There is a sweeping, crisscrossing shot of the ceiling.

"Wait," he says.

Then the screen goes black. It sounds as though the camera has been closed into a paper bag and dropped from an airplane. Cut to the bride and groom down the aisle. Zoom to lips locking under a pair of noses. Now the focus creeps back to reveal the newlyweds' faces.

Roland says, "This is it: the first kiss."

The couple kiss for a long time. The groom dips the bride and they sink into the bottom of the frame. Someone claps. Others join in.

"You don't think they kissed before this?" Luzzi says.

"It's the official kiss. It's the kiss people want to remember."

"What's on the other tapes?"

"I just want your opinion," Roland says. "Is the kiss important?"

"Probably, Roland. They just got married."

"See?" he says. And there it is: the dimpled chin, the pleading eyes. Here's the man who'd been a kid who cried in class at least once a month from kindergarten to graduation.

"See what?"

"I captured it. Why isn't that good enough?" He's looking away now, holding his head up, wiping his face with his palm.

"It's fine, Roland," Mr. Luzzi says. "Hey, I'm sure it'll be fine once you've edited."

"That's what I said to the client."

"You were hired to do this?"

"Yes. I need your help, Mr. Luzzi. Remember that time you did film club?"

Luzzi remembers. Roland was the only kid to sign up. They spent a semester of Friday electives in the media room watching classics: *Robin Hood, Babes in Toyland, The Taming of the Shrew.* "I'm not following you, Roland."

"I need the equipment in that room."

"Do you know it's summer now? School's out. You graduated, Roland. I'm on vacation."

"But the school's open, Mr. Luzzi. Summer G.E.D. I just need you to talk to your friends, so I have permission."

It's halfway through summer, and Mr. Luzzi hasn't lost his teacher paleness. Not enough time in the sun. Not enough time doing the things he said he would do this year. He's lost the momentum to run. He's been trying especially hard this past weekend, but on Friday night there was a power outage, so his alarm didn't go off Saturday morning. Then, on Saturday night, he was first awoken by glass breaking and people shouting somewhere in the neighborhood, and then there were sirens. The sirens came back later in the morning as the sun was rising on Sunday. After that, when his alarm clock radio went off in the middle of a lollipop jingle, Luzzi pulled it out of the wall and slept until noon. Now it was Monday, and instead of getting to his morn-

ing exercises and sitting down for a few hours at the word
processor, he was going back to the place he swore he'd not
think about until September.

They take his car.

"Did you ever finish that book you were writing?" Roland asks on the way. "The way I remember it, you were
going to be a writer. How is that going?"

"Well, I'm still working on it."

"I remember a story you read to us, Mr. Luzzi. It was
about a fat boy who committed suicide. I was confused, but
I liked it. I liked when you read to us in class. You read that
whole book to us once, remember? The one with the two
guys? That was by an actual writer. But I liked when you
read your stories, too. There was another story you wrote
about another suicide, but that one confused me as well. Are
all your stories about suicide?"

Luzzi knows the stories Roland's talking about. They
relied heavily on magical realism and dream logic, and the
characters were composites of students from his early years
of teaching. He thinks of himself as a composite, too, different characters inhabiting the same body, but sequentially.
He read somewhere once that over the course of seven years,
the cells in a body are completely replaced. Was Luzzi the
same person he was seven years ago? Fourteen years ago?
Twenty-one?

Did he still have that ambition in him? He'd lost track of
how many times he sent those stories out. He'd quit counting the rejections. He'd stopped stealing manila envelopes

from the main office. "No, they're not all about suicide," Luzzi says. "Just the ones I read to the class."

"And murder," Roland says. "That book you read ended with a guy murdering his friend. Reading is so depressing."

An Eagles song plays on the radio in the custodian's office at the far end of a distant hall. In the lobby, a security guard has Luzzi and Roland sign in and gives Roland a visitor pass.

"They fired one of us this morning," the guard says by way of small talk.

"What's that?" Luzzi says.

"They fired one of us. Drinking on the job. The guy on the sports field patrol. Now we'll be stretched thin. At least there'll be overtime."

"Sorry to hear that," Luzzi says, and walks off with Roland in search of Mr. Flatley.

"This is so weird," Roland says. "I never had to wear a visitor badge at school before."

Upstairs they find Flatley standing at a classroom door like a guard, either to discourage the young adults from leaving the room, or to keep others from coming in and passing judgment on his classroom management skills. English isn't Mr. Flatley's specialty. He teaches health in the regular school year. In his long career, he has always commuted from out of town. He has grown kids who were educated in another district, a wife with an office job in the city—a whole other life across the island kept separate from his job. For the past twenty years, he's worked through the summer in the dual role of G.E.D. principal and G.E.D. English exam instructor. He's teaching English now, using a collection of dittos from Luzzi's *Of Mice and Men* unit. Behind Flatley, the students have gathered their desks into a cluster and share a copy of Cliff's Notes.

"Did you hear what happened?" Flatley says when he sees Luzzi coming. Instead of the usual khaki pants, Flatley's white shirt is tucked into khaki shorts. He wears a full money clip in the shirt pocket like a badge.

"The drunk security guard?" Luzzi says.

"Jeff Ryans," Flatley says.

"Basketball Jeff?" Jeff Ryans is a student's name. "What happened to Jeff?"

"He was arrested at the gas station yesterday morning. Raving and naked. That's all the kids are talking about today, how Jeff went crazy on acid."

"You're kidding me," Luzzi says.

Roland is down the hall, pulling thumbtacks from a corkboard on the wall beside a classroom door.

Flatley says, "Can you believe it? That kid could've played for college if his head was in the right place."

"Jeff Ryans," Luzzi says to himself, and then he tries to recall the name of a kid from more than ten years ago, when he ran the alternative program, but all that comes to Luzzi is an acne-pocked sneer breaking into a fleeting smile. That kid could've ended up like Jeff Ryans. Any one of them could have.

"So, what are you doing here?" Flatley says. "It's your break." Then he looks down the hall to Roland. Roland is arranging the thumbtacks into a starburst pattern on the corkboard, his Pathmark shopping bag of videotapes on the floor at his feet.

"We need the media room," Luzzi says.

"Can I ask what for?"

"He's editing a video. I don't know. His father abandoned him. His mother died. Give the kid a break."

"You can't save them all," Flatley says. Then he looks over his shoulder to yell at the group of young adults in the classroom. "Five more minutes."

Luzzi has vague recollections of these young adults. They are kids who had failed to graduate this year, last year, the year before, kids who had dropped out or failed final exams, kids from broken homes who left high school to start broken homes of their own. But Luzzi remembers Jeff Ryans. Jeff Ryans is a poster child for the alternative program—a talented kid with a rough background and prone to violent emotional outbursts. Jeff Ryans was expelled the past year for kicking in a row of lockers and shattering the glass on the nurse's office door. It was all about a girl. Once upon a time, a kid like that would've been transferred to Luzzi's alternative program. Now they are simply sent packing.

"Sign him in," Flatley says, "but watch him with that equipment."

"Thanks," Luzzi says, and then he goes to escort Roland and his bag of tapes to the media room.

"Luzzi," Flatley says from his station in the doorway, "you got a price tag hanging off your shorts."

Without turning to give a hand wave of gratitude, Luzzi pulls the price tag off.

At the door to the media room, Luzzi tells Roland to take two hours. Then he goes to the teachers' lounge. The *New York Times* article is still framed on the wall, now hidden behind a filing cabinet. Luzzi takes the frame off the wall. TURNING "TOUGH KIDS" AROUND, the headline says. In the article, he finds the student's name he couldn't remember earlier. Jose Ramirez. Jose had dubbed Luzzi's alternative program the Emerald Forest. Soon, that's what all the kids were calling it. In a story Jose wrote for Mr. Luzzi's class, he had made Luzzi a character called the Luz. The story itself was called "The Luz." The unfinished work was, in total, a description of a teacher who wore a denim jacket on the weekend with the collar flipped up, his five o'clock shadow reaching half past the hour, sunglasses, cool hair. Luzzi liked the characterization. For the remainder of the writing assignment, he referred to himself as the Luz. Soon, all the kids in the Emerald Forest were calling Mr. Luzzi the Luz. The name stuck with him after Jose was released back into the main school the next year. The name followed him beyond the short life of the alternative program.

"The program, brainchild of English teacher Frank Luzzi, is regarded as unique because of the cooperation between the school district and the Youth Center, a community agency, which run the program jointly," said John Brady, director of the Suffolk County Criminal Justice Bureau, a county agency that assists programs aimed at reducing crime. The Floyd School District supplies the buildings and the teachers; the agency provides the social workers.

Luzzi takes the article out of the frame and makes a copy. Then he hangs it back on the wall. He helps himself to a Boston cream doughnut from a box next to the microwave. He pours a coffee.

The average gross adjusted income in Floyd Harbor is the lowest in the county, and most homes are headed by a single parent. Almost 25 percent of the families in the area have incomes below the poverty level. Half of the students in the area will have been involved with the courts by the time they graduate from high school—if they graduate—according to Pat Parker, project director for the Youth Center.

Halfway through his coffee, Luzzi stands in the doorway of his first classroom. Doors at either end open to adjacent classrooms. His plan had been to create an alternative program for troubled youth in the district. He got the backing of the superintendent. They made Luzzi principal of these three rooms. He ruled with benevolent, forgiving love.

"You can have the finest teachers in the world," said Sarah Prious, the program's social worker, "but if you can't talk about your feelings, you're going to be too bottled up to learn anything."

This is the kind of line Sarah would use on Luzzi after they were married for about a year. Luzzi was never going to grow as a person if he kept everything bottled up. He was never going to grow if he didn't expand his horizons beyond the kids in his classroom.

One of the problems with this population is they get no exposure, Sarah is quoted as saying in the article. *They think Port Jefferson is Manhattan. Leaving Floyd Harbor is out of their realm of reality.*

In the third year of the program, they were torn between Samantha and Shannon for a girl's name. When the baby died during birth, they named her Grace. Then the program was shut down. The article in the *Times* had given the program good publicity, but there had been no measurable proof of results.

The people here took us places, Jose Ramirez said. He'd come back for the day to be quoted for the article. *I feel homesick for the Emerald Forest, but it's not all that bad in the Dead World.*

Luzzi folds his copy of the article in four and stuffs it in the pocket of his shorts.

———

In the front lobby, heart of the Dead World, examples of exceptional student paintings hang high on the walls. In one painting that's been around since even before the Luz worked here, a man faces a wall the shade of blue that driftwood would be if driftwood were blue. The wall is also an ocean fading into sky with no clear horizon between them. The man is shirtless, and the tan on his back implies a serious relationship with the sun. A rough spot on his shoulder resembles a patch of sand. These details help in viewing the wall as an ocean. There's really nothing else to suggest it. The man's incredibly fleshed-out body, with bone structure and muscle under taut skin, thins and colors into manila around the lower back and elbows, and below that point he is paper-thin. Luzzi has to anchor his attention on the patch of sand, the tiny mole on the man's neck—something solid—or his attention slides right off the canvas.

Then Mr. Luzzi thinks for a moment about Roland, probably panicking in the media room, struggling with equipment he's never used before to complete a project beyond his capabilities. Luzzi thinks about Jeff Ryans, naked and handcuffed in the back of a Suffolk County police cruiser. Both kids are impossible to save.

In a few weeks, students will be herded in for another year. The beginning of a story about a high school basketball player will be filed away on Luzzi's word processor, the photocopy of the article buried in papers at home. He'll gaze at the painting in the lobby, again identifying with the phantom of a man staring into a blue void. Even before the first lesson begins, he'll have crossed the day off in his planner.

Far-Off Places

||||||||||||||||||||||||||||||||||||||||||||||||||||||||||||||||||||||||||||||||

"These hot dogs are the same as the ones at Floyd Harbor 7-Eleven," Rob said. "You like them, Jeff." Rob had eaten his hot dog before they left the parking lot of the 7-Eleven on Guy Lombardo Avenue in Freeport, where they had bought the sheet of acid.

Jeff's hot dog was still in its cardboard sleeve on the dashboard. He didn't take his eyes off the white lines of Sunrise Highway. He couldn't stomach a hot dog.

"Is this about Corrine?" Rob asked.

"I feel hollow inside."

"You need to eat something."

"The road is swaying."

"You need to eat. She's out having a good time. That's what we should do." It was obvious Jeff was not over Corrine, though he insisted the whole drive from Nassau County that he'd forgotten about her. After Corrine broke up with him, he had alluded to jumping off Smith Point Bridge with a weight on his ankle. He'd calmed down since then, but he wasn't back to his old self yet. Corrine was still a touchy subject. It was a mistake to mention her.

"How would you know what she's doing?"

"Hypothetical," Rob said. "Suppose. You know, there are other fish out there."

"Drop it already," Jeff said. "You don't know what you're talking about."

Scrub pine gave way to strip malls, signaling the approach of exit 58. Rob had nothing more to say about Corrine that would straighten Jeff out. The one thing he did know was that Corrine wasn't so great in any aspect that any guy she spurned should jump off a bridge. If that was the case, they both would be dead.

"Let's get some food and relax. How do you feel about that?"

"I can't breathe right," Jeff said. "Something's happening to my lungs."

"I don't feel anything. I think we got ripped off," Rob said. The last time they'd bought a sheet of acid and tested it to determine its worth, the streets of Floyd Harbor became canals like those in far-off and exotic places, showing them a murky image of themselves in traffic light as they peered from the curb into dark waters. Rob just didn't feel the flood coming this time. He wasn't feeling anything. He probably shouldn't have sold the four hits to Darrel Day at the 7-Eleven in Bellport. Darrel Day was in on something with Grady. If they thought Rob had ripped them off, there would be a price to pay.

The 7-Eleven was off by itself on William Floyd Parkway, about two miles from the Smith Point Bridge. The brightest thing at night, it attracted anything in the dark seeking a sign of life. The night the streets of Floyd Harbor were canals like those of far-off places, Jeff likened that 7-Eleven to a lighthouse. Rob said it was more like one of those big buoys with a light on it. Jeff said no, it was a lighthouse, it was far too big for a buoy, plus if it was a buoy it would be in the middle of a canal that they formerly knew as a street. Then Rob pointed out that the store was inside a parking lot and the parking lot was made of street material. Therefore, 7-Eleven was in the canal and so a buoy.

Whatever it was going to be tonight, Rob went inside, bought a hot dog, spooned sauerkraut on it, and put a single-serve packet of mustard in his shirt pocket.

"Eat this," Rob said to Jeff back in the car.

"What coin is this?" He held up a nickel.

"Five cents. Eat this hot dog."

"Give me a quarter."

"Eat first. Come on."

Unhappily, Jeff ate the hot dog. When he finished, Rob gave him a quarter. Then Jeff got out of the car and walked to the edge of the light, to the pay phone on the far end of the parking lot, way over by the parkway. He picked up the phone.

"That's not going to help you," Rob said, but Jeff dropped the quarter in and dialed. As Jeff huddled into the case of the pay phone, waiting, a man and a woman came from the shadows of one of those new homes stamped onto the woods that separated the store from a peopled neighborhood. Holding hands, the man and woman entered the parking lot's glow, the woman in a shiny purple dress, the man in red lifeguard shorts and sandals. As they entered the blinding store like fluttering moths, Rob saw a bigger picture of life as most people live it. Everybody has a light they strive toward. Corrine is Jeff's light, and having a great time is Rob's. That man and woman: the beer they carry out of 7-Eleven is their light, and they were drawn to 7-Eleven to get it.

Then, in a fit of laughter, Rob envisioned a man with a moth head in place of his own, spooning sauerkraut onto a hot dog in cackling fluorescent light.

Jeff was crying into the phone. He slammed the receiver. He pitched his car keys at the parkway and walked toward the car. He stopped, doubled over, and puked.

Rob opened his door. "What are you doing?"

One hand was on his knee, the other on his stomach.

Then Jeff was in the car. He seemed calm. "I know what's up. I know what's going on."

"We need those keys," Rob said.

———

From where Rob stood with his hot dog—by the 7-Eleven entrance, next to the measuring strip on the door that told his height (five-eight? nine?)—he could see Jeff tearing up the median grass between the lanes of the parkway. Jeff was serious about finding his keys.

"Hey, Jeff, do you want to finish this?"

"We'll never find the keys."

"Yes, we will!" Rob shouted back. He threw the hot dog at the garbage can for three points. It landed in the parking lot.

Jeff would have made that shot. Jeff would've played for the high school basketball team again, if not for getting kicked out when he broke a row of locker doors after seeing Corrine talking to another guy in the hallway. Jeff had also played in the summer at Teen Recreation Basketball Night in the beach parking lot. From the pavilion in the dunes that separate the parking lot from the beach, Rob had a view of all the good times at Teen Recreation. He'd warmed up to his role as spectator.

"We'll never find those keys," Rob said. The median grass lapped at his arms and neck. And funny how the daisies stamped onto his brain and multiplied, and Rob could watch them thrive with his eyes closed.

Jeff plucked grass by the fistful.

"There has to be a better way."

Jeff didn't answer. He kept tearing up the grass. Their spines ripped as though a wet mouth were biting down, sweeping back and forth.

"The ground is alive," Rob said. "You're killing it. Go look for your keys."

"The keys are in my pocket."

Rob opened his eyes. "You found them?"

"They were never lost."

"Oh. Let's go to the beach," Rob said. "I saw your car floating by the buoy, across the canal. I'll swim you there."

"Don't talk like that."

"I guess we don't have to worry about Darrel Day and Grady."

"I just want to talk to her."

"That's a bad idea, Jeff. Let's swim to the car. Then we'll drive to the beach."

"Stop saying that."

"Saying what?"

Jeff was standing now, pacing the median's valley. He looked at the keys in his hand. "You don't even know what's going on right now. Everything's a joke."

"Were you really on the phone with Corrine?"

"Just tell me what's going on," Jeff said.

"We're going to the beach is what, just like we planned before. There's nothing to worry about."

"You don't know how serious I am. Everything is changing."

"You need to relax. Try breathing. Try closing your eyes. See if you can still see me with your eyes closed."

Jeff paced, biting down on the knuckle of his pointer finger, and then he looked at Rob with an expression that said, "You know what? Let's just have a good time." Jeff's car started, and Rob opened his eyes. Jeff was pulling his blue Honda out of the 7-Eleven, in the opposite direction from the beach.

The 7-Eleven was neither a buoy nor a lighthouse. It was a small island. Rob was stranded.

"I told you not to call me anymore," she said.

"This isn't Jeff."

"I know who this is. My parents are sleeping. What do you want from me?"

"I'm the last man here."

"Jesus," she said, "what are you on?"

"Put Jeff on the phone."

"Are you retarded?"

"He didn't get there yet?"

"He's coming here?"

"He'll be here really soon."

"What's wrong with you?" she said. "Seriously, what's you guys's problem?"

"Tell Jeff I'm taking a swim to the beach. I'll meet him there."

"He's really coming here?"

"Tell him I said to relax. Don't tell him I called, though."

"He has to stop this. He's—shit, he's outside. Oh, great. This is so retarded."

"Why is everything retarded? Put him on the phone."

"My parents are sleeping," she whispered. "Shit, he's coming to the door."

"Put him on the phone."

She hung up on him again. Rob dropped another quarter in the slot and dialed. Her line was busy.

"Corrine is trouble," Rob said.

Two boys had entered the parking lot on bicycles.

"I heard that," said the bigger of the two. He wore a red bandana on his head. A purple spot marked his neck where someone had sucked on it. "My advice? Stay away from her. We're trying to have a good time now, but it's impossible. We can't find anyone to buy us beer."

Rob looked at the smaller kid for a while, trying to decide what kind of bird he looked like most.

"Can you get us some beer?" Bird Boy said after a while.

"Name your poison."

Bird Boy handed Rob a wad of singles. "Just get something cheap."

"Yeah," Bandana Kid said, "get whatever you can get."

In addition to its convenient hours of operation, its selection of ready-to-go meals, and its role as a beacon of life in the dead of night, the 7-Eleven was an excellent location for meeting like-minded people. Rob remembered when he was the age of those two kids, riding his bike to the convenience store with a fistful of dollars, trying to find the cool guy who would get him a sixer. He could envision human interactions, such as the quick exchange he'd just had with his new friends, as a continuous pattern throughout history. This was shown in the repetition of blue ocean waves crashing on the shore for all eternity. It was a natural and simple model, but stripped of its context in the actual world. If Rob factored in the sun turning ocean water into clouds, and clouds raining down on pastures to help grass grow, which was eaten by farm animals, and that those animals were ground into the hot dogs now displayed on the counter next to the register— hot dogs that would be consumed by humans, who were at the top of the food chain, each generation equal to one link, connected to the link that followed and that which preceded in an ever-growing lineage being dragged across time and space, then dragged, Rob wondered, by what?

"Hi, can I help you?" said the clerk. He interrupted the flow of Rob's thought.

Then there was a slap on the glass door behind him. It was Bandana Kid. He pointed at his wrist, and Bird Boy shrugged as though cold. The weather was pleasant enough. They were uncomfortable, they wanted Rob to hurry, and they were using charades to show it. Rob could almost see the watch and feel the chill in the air.

In the parking lot, Bandana Kid said, "Is this a joke?"

"This is a gift." Rob gave them each a hot dog.

"What about the beer?"

"What beer?"

Bandana Kid frowned. "What the fuck, man?"

"I have something better," Rob said. He kept the acid sheet in a 7-Eleven napkin he got that afternoon from that first 7-Eleven in Freeport.

"What is it?" said Bird Boy.

"I know what that is," Bandana Kid said. He held a hand out to Rob, and Bird Boy did the same. Rob gave them two each and took another himself.

A world flooded to the stars awaited those boys. Bandana Kid had been there before, but Bird Boy was taking his first flight. Rob marveled at how he pedaled after his friend down the street, their bodies tottering side to side and arms pumping, elbows out like wings. Then the glint of their bicycles vanished in a blink. Clouds had drifted into the sky, brighter than the night already buried in the distant past, way back to when Jeff and Rob were looking for the keys. Jeff had been gone forever. Would he return? Calling Corrine again as a way of reaching him was futile. But still Rob held the beeping pay phone to his head. Busy, busy. How did his fingernails get so dirty? The pink spatter of Jeff's eaten hot dog basked in the store light, and where Bandana Kid had pressed against the glass door, oily handprints gleamed—all markers of a time gone by, a night unreachable now except by two boys in their prime, pumping toward the setting moon. Night was leaving Floyd Harbor to rise above some far-off place where a police siren skittered like a cicada on a screen door. Maybe Rob should have perched on Bird Boy's handlebars and followed the pull of the moon, but the boys, by now, were long gone.

Rob got in the passenger seat. "Jeff? Jeff. Jeff, Jeff, Jeff." Rob had nothing else to say to him. He had forgotten where they'd left off.

"Everything's anew," Jeff said.

"What does it mean?" Rob said. "What are you looking at outside?"

"It's time to go." Jeff adjusted the rearview mirror. His hand was bloody.

"What happened there?"

"I put my hand in glass."

"At Corrine's house?"

"At her window."

"Jesus. There's blood on your pants."

Jeff looked at his hand.

"You need bandages."

"We need gas." A smile crept across Jeff's face, and then he laughed. "I was just thinking of all the meat I am, just meat running around with ideas in my head." He fiddled with the car's cigarette lighter.

"So, the thing going on with you and Corrine is what? What are we doing?"

"I thought we were going to the beach, no?"

———

Rob had to choose between a box of small bandages and a first-aid kit the size of a cinder block: one product too little, the other too much. The convenience store was not convenient at all. It contained only extremes. First Jeff, now this. The same with Corrine. She'd stopped looking like a little Hawaiian boy hop-scotching to the end of her driveway and advanced into the form of a woman on the corner watching high school boys swarm under a basketball net. She had breasts. She wore short shorts. That was the day Rob laid down thirty dollars for the player who could hit the most three-pointers in a row. Rob told Corrine he almost didn't recognize her. She looked grown up. She smiled.

"Hi," the clerk said.

Rob stood at the register.

"Someone get hurt?"

"Yes," Rob said. "My friend who threw up a hot dog before is now bleeding."

"He's vomiting blood?"

"No."

"Okay," the clerk said. "Just the kit? No hot dog this time?"

"What hot dog?"

"You always buy a hot dog."

"No, not this time. What do I owe you?"

The kit scanned to fifteen dollars, way too expensive.

"Just give me some napkins instead."

"You need to buy something to get napkins. Maybe he needs a hospital?"

"I did buy something," Rob said, and he gave an account of each occasion, working his way back to the stop at the 7-Eleven on the way home from Nassau County, where Rob bought the first hot dog and took only the one napkin he needed. To that, the clerk said Rob needed to make a new purchase, that in the time between when Rob last bought something and now the window of napkin-getting had closed.

"That doesn't seem fair."

"You hang out here all night, you throw your trash around. Your friends dirty the glass. Who cleans it? Who cleans the parking lot?"

"Fine," Rob said. "I'll buy a hot dog."

Jeff knocked on the door. He cupped his bloody hand against the glass and searched Rob out, blinded by the store light. This was a threshold he did not wish to cross.

"See. This is what I'm talking about," the clerk said.

"But now I'm buying a hot dog," Rob said, and he shoved a stack of napkins in his pocket.

"How many of those did you eat tonight?" Jeff said in the parking lot.

"I bought this one for you," Rob said, putting the hot dog on the dashboard and digging the napkins out of his pocket.

"No way. I'm not eating that."

"I don't expect you to eat it. Hold these with your fist." He put the napkins in Jeff's murky hand. It was impossible to make sense of the cut with the blood gathered around it.

"I can't make a fist."

"You're not trying."

"I can't feel my fingers. I feel sick just looking at that thing."

"Don't look. Do you have tape?"

"I'm slipping back in time. How bad am I bleeding?"

"I just need something to use as tape, and then we can get back to normal. Do you have any tape?"

"I don't know," Jeff said. "Look in the trunk."

The rear bumper sticker said I LIVE IN FLOYD HARBOR. In the trunk Rob found a pair of high school basketball shorts, a length of chain, a cinder block, and a roll of duct tape in a black plastic bag. It was the tape Jeff had used to reattach the back bumper, the kind of tape that fixes everything. What a welcome sight.

Back in the car, Rob taped the wound. "Change your pants for these shorts."

But instead of changing, Jeff said, "I want you to throw that hot dog away."

"We'll save this one for the beach," Rob said. He had a feeling now that he'd been waiting all night to go to the beach. At night, the ocean was a deep unknowable mystery as wide as the sky, and Rob could stand at its edge. He was ready for something so grand.

"Na-uh."

"If it's a problem, I'll put the hot dog in the glove box."

"It's not the hot dog."

"You're not in your right mind. Let's get out of this light. Maybe she has the cops after you. I heard sirens before when I was on the pay phone."

"Who did you call?"

"Okay, she didn't call the cops, but she's really upset with you. You need to give her space. You need to think. That's why you should go to the beach. You can meditate there. It's the best place for you to be right now—thinking and meditating and straightening out."

"I don't know how to meditate."

"Just close your eyes and breathe deep, like this." A universe of cream-colored, hot-dog-patterned wallpaper blew through Rob's mind, and then the car was moving. Jeff wore his golden basketball shorts. They were going in the direction of the beach.

"You can meditate," Jeff said. "I'm shooting hoops."

Rob was glad to hear this. Jeff playing basketball was like a fish finding water. He was a natural. Jeff was the one who had hit seven three-point shots in a row and won Rob's thirty dollars that fateful day.

"Don't call me anymore," Corrine had said. "Okay? Don't say anything to Jeff. I'm sorry."

Rob didn't tell Jeff. Whatever reputation Corrine had

gotten, she earned on her own. What was it Bandana Kid heard about her? Rob should have asked him, but he and Bird Boy were somewhere far off in Mastic Beach, in that tangled string of yellow dots across the bay. Lights on the Smith Point Bridge looked like a roller coaster. The ocean called, and the basketball court on the far corner of the lot was lit like a stage under the tall question mark of a lamppost.

"Are you playing?"

"This is where," Jeff said. "Right here I kissed her the first time."

"No," Rob said, "you kissed her over there, near the bridge."

"I meant in general," Jeff said, "in this area."

"Hey, guess what? I already sold four of these." Rob's pocket was empty. In the other pocket he had a few dollars, in his shirt pocket a packet of mustard. "Jeff, can we go back?"

Jeff's eyes were closed.

"I lost it, Jeff. We need to go back."

"There's no going back." Jeff looked far way. He took small sips of the salty air. "My skin is too dry." This must have been around the time Jeff decided he was turning into a fish. Or had his transformation started earlier in the night? Whatever put the idea in his head? When Rob later found Jeff's car parked at the apex of the bridge, he thought his friend had followed through with his ridiculous threat to drown himself. He couldn't know Jeff took a dive, swam across the bay, turned up naked at the gas station on Neighborhood Road, and was wrestled into the back of a police cruiser.

All Rob knew now was that he had to see the ocean. He had waited long enough. What else could he do? Walk the two miles to 7-Eleven? The clerk would come out to clean the parking lot and throw the napkin in the trash. Only Rob had put the acid napkin in his pocket, hadn't he? Where was it?

Where was the moon? Time had slipped away. His ankles sank into sand, and the ocean licked his feet like a tame, idiotic giant. A salty mist whetted his appetite. Rob wished he'd remembered to take that hot dog with him. He was being so forgetful. He was careless. A string of sauerkraut had dried on his shirt. He had that mustard in his pocket. Its tang washed down the sauerkraut and then coated a hollow space inside him. He could feel it in his tear ducts. It wasn't a good feeling at all.

Fatta Morgada

||||||||||||||||||||||||||||||||||||||||||||||||||||||||||||||||||||||||||||

Suicide was planned for Thanksgiving. Stuffed turkeys filled ovens. Biscuits sweated in warm bowls. Corn bread burned. Marshmallows bubbled and browned on yams. Potatoes softened, gravy thickened, butter dripped from boiled corn, cranberry sauce chilled, and wine breathed, waiting to be poured—all far from Ricardo Morgada. Shower steam collected in drops on his walls, clouded the doorway, and spread into the hall. The water beat so hot it felt as though the roll of neck would melt into his shoulders. He drew the razor over his chin, nicking off the last bit of stubble. All his facial hair gathered in a clump by the drain. He shut the water off, stepped out of the tub, and stood in front of the medicine cabinet, concentrating on his breathing. His olive skin was tinged red, and the razor burn itched where his skin folded: neck and chin, where his cheeks met his mouth. Pull back his cheeks to his ears, and the picture of his sun-reddened father pinned to the bedroom wall could have been mistaken for Ricardo. The picture was taken twenty years earlier, when Ricardo was a baby. His father, Ricardo Morgada, Sr., had just docked *Mujer de las Aguas* for the first time. Ricardo's mother had snapped the picture from the dock. His father stood on the bow with the August sun on his face, his thick hair caught in a salty breeze.

There were aspirin, cotton swabs, laxative, toothpaste, sinus pills, Valium, multivitamins, asthma meds, a hair clip, a few bobby pins, and nail clippers in the medicine cabinet. The hair accessories and the Valium belonged to Meredith, the volunteer from St. Jude's who did Ricardo's shopping, prepared meals, and kept the house in order. She also kept a bottle of brandy under the sink. Fatta took the aspirin, the Valium, the brandy, the asthma medication, and a tall glass of water into his mother and father's old bedroom. He sat on the floor naked and caught his breath as he placed the bottles of medication on the floor around him, the way he'd sit on the floor to put his pants on. Then he took a sip of the water, slipped a Valium between his lips, drank a swig of brandy, and chased it with a sip of water. He did the same with the asthma meds. He finished the brandy. He took two aspirin and then started again with the Valium. He alternated pills until he finished the glass of water.

When he lay down, his weight spread over his frame. He felt pinned to the floor. The room was as his parents had left it. There was a thick black cross on a beige wall, clothes in the closet, statues of saints on shelves, and on the shorter dresser, relics from a life they lived in Mexico before his time. On the taller dresser, there was a framed dollar bill from his father's first pay as a migrant laborer on a potato farm, farther east on Long Island. His first seasonal clamming license was also framed, taking the space between the dollar and the document that certified him as a marine engines mechanic. A green rotary phone sat quietly on the shorter dresser. Ricardo's mother, Mercedes, had spent hours talking on that phone. She was there the day he came home from a high school field trip with a dark purple bruise on his cheek and wet pinkish eyes. When Ricardo walked into the room, Mercedes said, "Ricky, who did this to you? *Hilda, lo llamo mas tarde.*" She hung up the phone and took Fatta by the hand. "Tell me who did this."

Rob Lane was the one who hit his face, but they all did it. The guidance department had arranged a field trip to the technical school for students planning on blue-collar futures, students who would not go to university. Ricardo wanted to be a mechanic or a chef. He was the only one from his special class on that bus because it was the only bus with an aisle-facing seat—one that he could fit into without too much trouble. Boys in the back whispered and laughed, looked over their seats and stole glances at Ricardo. On the way back from the trip, someone said, "His name is Ricky the Retarded Spic." Everyone laughed. The chaperone was talking to the bus driver, oblivious.

Someone else said, in their best Speedy Gonzales, "There ain't no one fatta than Reee-car-doh More-gah-da."

"He's Fatta Morgada," someone else said. Ricardo pursed his lips around his inhaler, his eyes fixed on the window across from him, and imagined walking down the street they were on, watching the bus flash by, the faces of those boys a blur.

Rob Lane stood in front of Ricardo's seat with his back to him and said, "Now I present to you Ricardo 'the fatta than anyone, retarded Special Ed spic' Morgada!" He swung his hand back and his fist caught Ricardo's face, and Ricardo's head banged against the metal bar on the window behind him. No one called him Chubba or Fatso after that. They all called him Fatta Morgada.

An hour had passed. Ricardo didn't feel anything but the effects of a single dose of his asthma medication—the quickened thump of his heart, the stirring in his stomach, the dull pain in his head. How would it look if they could see him like this, naked and fat on the floor with all the pills around him, but still breathing? If they found him like this, they would all have another good laugh. But if he was dead, then he'd just be dead. He needed to take more pills. He needed more water.

He struggled to get up. When he finally did, everything in the room seemed to shrink into the corners, and then the corners bulged. Ricardo stumbled to the bathroom doorway, feeling his body moving forward and then held back momentarily by his weight. He stepped sideways through the doorway, the naked skin of his torso touching the molding on both sides. In the bathroom, something slapped like waves against a boat. Water dripped from the showerhead into a shallow pool in the tub. A clump of his hair stopped the water at the drain. Ricardo steadied himself with one hand on the wall, reached into the tub to close the faucet tight, and as he was about to lean over, his eyes fixed on the window—the dirt road, the shriveled entanglement of grapevines beyond that wove through a rusty chain-link fence—and he remembered summers as grapes, as warm fish innards and seaweed drying on the dock in the afternoon heat. On the dock, Fatta used to sit with his father and struggle with the raw chicken parts between his stubby fingers as he tried to anchor the meat in the wiry snare of his crab trap.

Farther out, in the cold bay, beyond the fence and beyond the dock, a naked woman backstroked. He could not make out her face nor tell the color of her skin. She was a ripple in his vision that distorted the background, like looking through an empty water glass. But she was intricate, and she moved as real as any woman he had ever seen. In one easy, flowing motion, she slipped through the water into a belly-down position and arched the bottom of her back so that her head and neck delved into the water. Her buttocks followed, moving forward and sinking, and her legs lifted from the water and disappeared straight downward, leaving behind a gentle ripple in the unusually calm bay.

Ricardo stepped into the tub and pressed his forehead

against the window to get a wider view of the bay. He wanted to see her again, but everything was still. His eyes strained to take it all in, to see if a breeze would break the calmness of the water or brush a dead leaf from a branch. Just dive in, he thought. Just turn and go and dive in after her. It's not that hard, because she is waiting for you to turn and go and go down and drown. He felt himself slipping before he slipped in the tub and kept falling farther into wet dark until his falling slowed to floating, and he opened his eyes under the sun-glazed surface of the bay.

He drifted down. His soles touched the floor of the bay, sank into the muck until it covered his toes, and then he rose until he was suspended in the middle of the water. He felt the current of a passing body and he reached out for it. He missed. All around him was dark except the distant glare on the surface. He panicked for a second when he thought he might soon feel fearful of drowning, but it was a fleeting fear. At that moment, numbness trailed down his spine. He turned and caught her by the hand, pulling her in. She glided forward, resting her waist against his belly and her free hand against his chest. Her hair moved slowly through the water and wrapped around his head, tickling his ears. The tip of her nose brushed against his, and he was overcome with calmness. He felt her hair sliding over his head when she drifted downward and pressed her nose against his parting lips. She continued down, tracing his body with her hands, taking in his pain until the tips of her fingers left his toes.

Ricardo couldn't feel his body after that, but his mind was as wide as the bay. She swam through it with strong, lulling swiftness. She dove deep to where the weeds grew, and she tore them by the roots with a sweeping rip tide she created from the vigor of her speed. But she quickly tired. She drifted upward and toward the shore, broke through the surface and gasped. She crawled out and waded, leaning with her hands on her knees, the cool water dripping from her body.

With each drip, Ricardo felt himself coming together. Each drip reverberated in the water, and with each he grew more aware: aware of his limbs, of floating up, of his body getting cold. His lungs. Ricardo Morgada was pale in the face, his eyes just over the surface.

There was a boat on the horizon, across the wide bay, across the ripples and the placid sandbars, past the seaweed patches and just inside the choppy inlet that split Fire Island. Freezing water rushed into the side of the boat, tilting the bow, pulling the *Mujer de las Aguas* under. Wood cracked against the large stones that lined the edges of the inlet. He heard the cries of his mother. He heard his father yell for help. Then water dripped on his forehead. Another drop. Another. One more drop formed at the tip of the shower-head. The left side of his chest and his arm had gone numb, wedged together in the tub, and his right arm and leg hung over the outer edge. He heard the familiar sound of Meredith's station wagon pulling into the driveway.

The Shaft

IIIIIIIIIIIIIIIIIIIIIIIIIIIIIIIIIIIIIIIIIIIIIIIIIIIIIIIII

In 1965, when the south peninsula of Floyd Harbor was still officially named Mastic Beach, a '57 Chevy plowed into two parked cars on a backstreet. Sal imagines the Chevy as baby blue with a single white pin stripe. He imagines his father, Jim Lenton, the driver of the car, standing before the bench at the Suffolk County Court. Jim is a boy of eighteen, his hair slicked back with Vaseline. He wears tight black jeans. His leather shoes with pointed tips shine brighter than the polished wood floor of the courtroom. Sal's grandfather is there, staring at the back of Jim's greasy head.

A path cutting through a field somewhere in Vietnam closely resembles the backyard of Sal's childhood. He feels the presence of his father behind him, the smell of a Marlboro, the red-and-black flannel Jim wears moving into Sal's peripheral vision, always at the edge of his sight. Sal is in a procession of thirty soldiers, all marching in place on this path where a kiddie pool with sparkling water floats by just above the ground, and a clothesline with clothes pins throws a thin shadow over each man's face as it moves down the line. Always up ahead is the blue '57 Chevy, nudged into the sides of two parked cars.

Sal stares at the back of the shaved head of a man who is marching in front of him. The voice of Sal's father whispers, "That's Pete. The guy behind you is Smitty."

Smitty has a big smile on his face. He squints from the sun so hard that his eyebrows almost touch.

Smitty says, "Hey, Pete. Got a letter from Rachel, the nurse with red hair. She'll be my wife, you bet. We'll have a bar in Texas."

Sal smiles at Smitty and then faces forward.

Jim whispers to Sal, "Your mother will be my wife. There's that letter." A piece of paper appears in Sal's hands. There are hearts inked in the margin and round, bubbly letters from the top of the page to the bottom. Little circles dot the i's. "It smells like her perfume. She put lipstick on just to kiss it. Think about that."

Sal sees his mother kissing the paper in her bedroom on Cranberry Drive. Her hair curls upward and out at her shoulders. Her eyes are closed. Then there are two loud bangs followed by two thumps. She opens her eyes and turns to the sound.

The whole line of soldiers, except for Pete and Smitty,

disappears into the heavy jungle along the trail. Sal stands between Pete and Smitty in air so thick it holds him in place. Pete and Smitty have dropped to their knees and are about to fall over. Thick clouds of dust rise around their legs and thin out by their waists. Blood trickles from their temples, drips from their chins in heavy drops, and then hits the ground, creating little spurts of dust clouds inside the larger clouds dissipating in the air surrounding the kneeling soldiers.

"What do you do?" Jim's singing voice whispers. "One, two, three soldiers all in a row. One, two bullets. Three? Three? Three?"

"What are you going to do?" another voice demands. Sal turns to a field full of polished mahogany-colored grass like so many long splinters of wood sticking in the ground. At the near edge of the field sits the Suffolk County judge behind an old wooden desk. His hair is white, and his skin is loose on his face. Behind the judge, at the far edge of the field, there stands the Veterans Memorial from Bald Hill in Farmingville—an elongated white pyramid. Around the top, the American flag is painted on an angle, the way a real flag hangs on a pole on a windless day. The sky is a shiny, baby blue. A green plane flies overhead, leaving a streak of white across the sky.

The judge says, "What are you going to be? Criminal or hero? Look at your father, Jim. Look at his face. Does he want a criminal for a son, or is he the father of a hero?"

Jim whispers, "I stole and broke that blue car. It was jail or the service. They gave me a choice."

"Look at your father, Jim," the judge says.

Sal looks at his grandfather, Jim's father.

Jim's father says, "I always liked the Marine uniform."

Thirty soldiers march in place. A kiddie pool floats by and a clothesline passes overhead. When it passes over Sal's head, he hears his mother sing, "Who are the people in your neighborhood? Sal, who are the people in your neighborhood?"

Sal is small and wet in the kiddie pool, and his mother is hanging white socks on the clothesline. The day is a blue sky with no wind. Inside the house, a TV is on.

Sal's mother says, "Sal, go inside and see your father."

Sal comes out of the pool and goes inside. In the dark living room his father sits on the blue couch by the stairs. His hair has grown into unkempt shag. A full beard softens his jawline, and his belly rests a few inches over his belt.

Jim looks at his son and lights a cigarette. The flame from the match brings out a yellow tint in his bloodshot eyes.

Sal sits on his father's lap.

An old man on the TV says, "Is there a hero in you?"

Sal grabs the remote control and changes the channel to PBS. They watch *Sesame Street*. Sal can see his father's red-and-black flannel in the corners of his sight. Smoke from the Marlboro saunters in front of his face. Empty bottles of Budweiser cover the coffee table.

Cookie Monster appears on the screen and says, "*Sesame*

Street was brought to you today by the color blue, the letters A, W, O, and L, and the numbers one, two, and—"

Two shots are fired. It startles Cookie Monster and he quickly turns his head. Smitty and Pete drop to the ground, their faces expressionless and their knees in the dirt. Blood runs down their dirty necks and flows underneath their green shirts.

Jim, whispering in Sal's head, sings, "Pete was a person in my neighborhood."

On a green plane flying over a mahogany field like a sea full of driftwood waving in the wind, Pete sits in a green cadaver bag. Sal is sitting next to him.

The pilot, who is the judge with a head of white hair from Suffolk County Court, says, "Peter, young Peter, are you a criminal or are you a hero? The court wants to know."

Sal can barely make out the judge's words over the roar of the engine.

"I'm not a criminal, sir," Pete says, his voice also drowned out by the engine, muffled even further by the cadaver bag.

"You were in the car, Peter. You didn't steal it, you didn't drive, but you were there. You and Jimmy."

"Sir, I'm not a criminal." Peter's head bleeds through the bag. The blood spreads on the fabric.

"Peter, look at Jimmy," the judge says.

The cadaver bag shifts toward Sal.

"That boy is going to be a hero."

Sal turns away and looks through the window. His reflection on the glass is translucent, his features slipping in and out of focus. As the plane flies past the Veterans Memorial on Bald Hill, his father's face comes together on the window, staring back at him. Sal says, "Look, Dad. The Veterans Memorial."

"Yeah," Jim whispers. His face disappears as Sal focuses on the tall white structure with the painting of the flag draped around the tip. "We call it the Shaft."

The judge comes out of the cockpit and hands Sal a shovel with a spade head. He draws a rectangle on the floor of the plane with a piece of chalk.

Pete says, "Jim, my friend, are you going to dig my grave?"

Jim tells Sal to start digging, and he does. The metal floor of the plane rips like foil. Sal scoops up a heaping mound of dirt. Jim whispers, "Yeah, I dug his grave."

The airplane lands. Sal steps out into his father's bedroom in Floyd Harbor, blisters on his hands and traces of dirt up to his elbows.

Sal's mother is there, facing the wall, kissing a piece of paper with her eyes closed. She turns around and looks at Sal. "Jimmy, you've been AWOL for thirty days. You have to go back. If you don't, they'll put you in jail."

Sal turns around to his father's bed.

His grandfather is sitting there. His grandfather says, "Jimmy, what are you? Are you a criminal, or are you a hero?"

Sal's mother grabs his hand and says, "It's not your fault, Jimmy. You didn't force Pete into that baby-blue '57 Chevy."

CITATION . . . On 17 March 1969 while his unit was deployed at the An Hoa Combat Base the encampment came under a heavy volume of hostile rocket fire and several Marines were seriously wounded. Disregarding his own safety, Lance Corporal Lenton unhesitatingly moved about the terrain to render first aid to wounded comrades and assist in the expeditious medical evacuation of the casualties. Constantly concerned with the combat readiness of his unit, he tirelessly trained his men and molded them into an effective fighting force. Lance Corporal Lenton's leadership, professional competence, and steadfast devotion to duty reflect great credit upon himself, the Marine Corps, and the Naval Service.

Was Corporal Jim Lenton aware of his right to be defended by a civilian lawyer, provided by him at no expense to the government? Did he desire to proceed with his defense counsel, provided by the United States free of charge?

Was that Corporal Lenton's request in writing for trial by military judge alone? Had his counsel delineated the difference between a court-martial with jury members and one composed of a military judge alone? Did he understand that the judge alone would determine his guilt or innocence? Did he understand that the judge alone would sentence him, should he be found guilty?

Did Jimmy know that by his plea of guilty to the charge of Unauthorized Absence he waived—and by waived the judge meant gave up (in case Jimmy didn't know)—his right against self-incrimination, even if Jimmy believed he was guilty, putting the burden of proof on the prosecution? Was Jimmy aware that his *right against self-incrimination* was his *right to say nothing at all*? Did Jimmy understand the meaning of *waive*?

If Jimmy now understood the charge of Unauthorized Absence to which he had pleaded guilty, then the judge was ready to ask Jimmy questions. These questions, the judge said, were called the facts.

"How old were you when you came in?"

"Nineteen, sir."

"How much time did you spend in Vietnam?"

"A full tour, sir."

"At the completion of your tour, were you authorized some leave?"

"Yes, sir."

"And you were married during this leave?"

"Yes, sir."

"At the end of that leave you were supposed to come back to the Second Marine Division?"

"Yes, sir."

"Now, you've been convicted of a very long period of unauthorized absence—about thirteen months. Do you realize all this is bad time?"

"Yes, sir."

Two thumps echo up the stairs. Sal is startled. He looks back and forth between his mother and grandfather. Then he pulls his hand from his mother and goes down the stairs to find Smitty and Pete dying in the darkness. Their blood fills the niches in the wood floor and floods the cracks between the planks. A hypodermic needle filled with a cloudy, yellowish liquid is on the banister. It glows like a dim lightbulb, drawing out only the brighter colors in the room and making everything look soft. Jim tells Sal to stick the needle in his arm. He does.

"What is this?" Sal asks.

"That's piss."

"Why am I putting piss in my bloodstream?"

"Because it hurts to bleed, son. Did it ever hurt to piss?"

The stairs turn into a path in Vietnam that looks much like the backyard of Sal's childhood. Dust settles on the ground and all is quiet. Twenty-seven soldiers crawl from the sides of the trail and check the two bodies lying in the path. Someone says, "We have a breather. Where's the morphine?" They huddle around Pete, whose breathing is hard and shallow. His eyes are fixed on the blue sky, where an airplane trails a white streak. His breath sounds like a faraway scream.

Jim whispers, "Pete needs piss in his bloodstream."

———

Sal's mother, Meredith, takes the stand.

"Is the accused in this case your husband?"

"Yes, sir."

"Are you expecting a child at this time?"

"Yes, I am."

"If your husband has to go to the brig, where will you live during that time?"

"I found a place in Mastic Beach, New York."

"And how will you support yourself?"

"I have no idea."

"What did you think of him coming into the Marine Corps?"

"He'd been in some trouble. I thought the service would be good for him."

A soldier pulls two cadaver bags from a green canvas bag. When he unzips one, a pulley squeaks. A thin shadow passes over Sal's eyes. There is a shovel in his hand, traces of dirt up to his elbows, and the hot sun in the clear blue sky beats down on his neck. Sweat drips from his chin.

His mother says, "Sal." She is hanging clothes on the line. "Sal, your father wants to see you when you're finished digging that hole."

A bang comes from inside the house. Sal and his mother turn to look. Sal drops the shovel and runs inside.

The TV is on, and its glow fills the room with pulsing blue. The man in the foreground on the screen is an old man in a Marine uniform. He has gray hair and his skin hangs loose on his face. There are two dead bodies on the ground in the background, blood oozing from their heads and spreading out on the dusty path. An airplane screeches across the bluest sky, leaving a trail of white as thin and straight as a pin stripe.

The old man says, "Is there a hero in you?"

The camera pans up close on the dead bodies and focuses on the expressionless faces.

Another voice says, "The few. The proud. The Marines."

In the bedroom, above the living room where Sal stands, drips of Jim's blood, mixed with piss, drop from the soaked edge of the blue comforter on Jim's bed, steadily tapping the floor. Sal ascends the stairs, quietly, hearing his own heart and breath now, and the drip, the stairs creaking, all the time knowing what he will find behind his father's door but afraid to look. And at the door he just stands there. He stares at the doorknob. Then he feels his father's hands on his shoulders, his eyes still fixed on the door, his mind still on what lies beyond.

"Three soldiers in a row, Sal. One, two, three. Three, Sal."

Animal Kingdom

We met at the table of third cousins and estranged friends. A champagne toast and beers later, Rose slipped to me the controversial pregnancy behind the whole production.

"Really?" I said. "Keith's a dad?"

"*Someone's* a dad," Rose said. I pressed her for details. She said she would never tell on the bride. She and Rebecca were blood. She sealed her mouth by twisting an imaginary key in the lock of her pursed lips.

The next morning, I told Rose she looked more like a Betty. It was all the tattoos, stamped here and there like cargo tags on a well-traveled suitcase—a star on her sternum, a tribal sun on her neck, Chinese characters on her wrists. It would be nearly ninety degrees when the cat fell on her, but now the sun was just a dusty block of light on my bedroom wall.

"How'd you know I like the name Betty?" she said.

"I can read your mind."

"Oh yeah?" she said. "What do I want for breakfast?"

We put our wedding clothes back on and walked to Neighborhood Road. A man in red shorts I later learned was my neighbor a few houses down smiled at Rose and saluted us. I would come to hate this man in a few hours, but right now he was just another resident of Mastic Beach. Right now, I looked forward to two eggs rolled over, bacon, and cheese on a toasted kaiser, squirt of ketchup, salt and pepper, orange juice, coffee regular. Rose copied my order, and by the time we left Handy Pantry with those sandwiches, the sun hung heavy in the power lines, ready to drip. Outside Handy Pantry, by the trash bin, two guys who looked like they had been up all night ate their sandwiches and read the classifieds.

"I'd like to eat these eggs at the beach," I said, moments before the cat dropped. We were back on my block. Leafy branches arched overhead. "I'd like a picnic on the sand with you, Rose, next to a family with lots of kids running around, and later, I don't know, take a swim somewhere. That's the mood you put me in."

"Me, too," Rose said. "I used to have picnics all the time.

Volleyball, drinks." She stopped walking and grabbed my elbow. "We should do that, Dan! That would be fun, cocktails and volleyball on the beach."

The cat high up in the tree was lucky we stopped there the moment he couldn't hold on anymore. When it landed on Rose's chest, she screamed.

"I thought they landed on their feet," I said. I'd found a shoebox for the cat and left it on my step. Rose and I stood at the screen door, watching his shallow breaths. He was sucked nearly bloodless with fleas, his tongue and gums as paper-white as his fur. He was a grown-up kitten, around the age when cats jump at everything that moves. Rose lost her appetite after seeing all those fleas rolling like poppy seeds under his white fur, but I was hungry. I ate my sandwich. It didn't seem right to talk about how good the eggs were, so I enjoyed my breakfast in silence at the door, wondering whether the eyes were naturally yellowish, or was that another condition the cat suffered?

"Oh, the poor thing," Rose said, face against the screen. "Dan, we can't let him die like this."

I'm no animal hater. I kicked a dog only once, a sneaky mutt who'd come up behind me and nipped my ankle when I was walking down the street. The dog didn't even bark, just bit and looked at me like I was the stupid one. Except for that dog, the animal kingdom is fine by me. But what is the life of a cat worth unless you're the cat? Cats die every day.

"I don't want that cat to suffer any more than you do," I said.

Rose found my hand on her hip and squeezed. "Are we taking him to the animal hospital?"

How does a woman bend the world to her will like that? Sure, I had known Rose for less than a day, but I already envisioned myself permanently seated next to her on some porch swing of the future. I thought I'd never let it happen again. But this time, with Rose, I felt ready to roll the dice, for no other reason than the dumb luck that had been following me around all summer. In June I'd answered correctly on the *Rockin' Radio* call-in show that the Germans did not attack Pearl Harbor, and I was awarded a hundred bucks and a giant thermos. Then I qualified for unemployment and sold the crappy boat Keith had ended up giving me instead of the money he owed for the landscaping work. He said he needed that money to buy a new lawn mower, a weed whacker, and rakes to replace the ones that were stolen from the van. A week later, on my way to turn in a winning scratch-off worth fifty bucks, a dentist pulled up in his Cadillac and offered me a day job. The dentist had forgotten his office keys and wanted me to slip my skinny ass through the basement window of his practice, feel my way through the dark, up the stairs, and find the door that opened to the parking lot. When I opened that back door to bright daylight, his patients applauded me. They'd been waiting all morning. It was ten minutes of actual work, and I was paid thirty dollars for it.

And now Rose had dropped into my life. I wasn't even expecting an invitation to that wedding, considering how Keith and I had left things off, but there I was at the reception, partaking in a ceremony of flowers and a garter with this woman, this Rose—a ceremony akin to an actual wedding of our own—followed by a honeymoon back at my place, a consummation, and now, I guess, a cat that needed a flea dip. It was a family-type situation.

"I guess I'm going to the pet store," I said. It was the right thing to say. I couldn't afford a vet.

When the phone company discontinued my service, I learned that the chances of quickly getting a taxi were good if I waited in front of Salty's on Neighborhood Road. But if you got in the wrong cab, look out, you're going everywhere. The blue hatchback from Harbor Coach—the car I finally caught—had a bumper sticker on the passenger door that said I LIVE IN FLOYD HARBOR. In a few minutes, it turned down a street that I first thought was a long driveway but led to a cluster of little red houses with their own driveways. I'd never been to this enclave. We picked up a frazzled young lady with four kids. The kids squeezed in the back with me while the lady rode shotgun. It took a few minutes of struggling to buckle the sleeping baby's car seat. The two little girls were dripping in frilly bathing suits, and the oldest kid, a boy, about ten and twiggy like his mom, wore jeans and a black tank top. He sat next to me. I could tell the mom cut the kids' hair. Their bangs were slanted on the same angle.

The driver put the car in gear and drove.

"Mom," the boy said, "it's hot out. I'm hot."

"Shut up!" the mom said. "Just shut up already! You forgot your bathing suit. Am I supposed to dress you?"

"Sorry," the boy said.

"I just want everybody to get off my case," the mom said.

"I said I'm sorry."

"You're sorry," she said, doubtful. She lit a cigarette and turned to the driver. "Make a left up there."

The driver flicked her left-turn signal. I was about to say that, since I was picked up first and since left was opposite of the direction I needed to go, we should figure out a better, more fair way to make this trip we were on, but then the boy, who was staring hard at the back of his mom's head, reached over and pinched the thigh of one of his sisters. Before the girl even finished her yelp, the mom, instantly hanging over the back of the seat, slapped the girl and whacked the boy's face. Her ashes dropped on my pants. The cabby took the turn. The kids' arms flailed to block the slaps too late. They erupted in tears, touching their faces. The girl who wasn't hit joined their crying.

"I've had enough of you two! Christ! This is why we can't go anywhere." She edged back down into her seat, stared at them for a moment, and then faced forward and huffed. "God, I can't handle these kids. Jesus. Man."

The baby slept.

"I want to go home," cried the girl who wasn't hit.

"We are going home. Cry all you want about it."

That sad family got out of the cab at a house hidden behind wild hedges and a jungle lawn on another street that looked like a long driveway.

They were not the family I'd imagined having a picnic next to at the beach.

"I should call CPS," the driver said. She drove to the corner stop sign. Her side of the front seat was sunken to the shape of her body, bulging in the back.

"I'm going to the pet store," I reminded her.

"Yeah," she said, looking at me in the rearview. She'd been crying. She looked like she'd been crying for days. "Oh, mother, not this kid."

I turned around to see the kid. But the kid, a he-man with a glossy shaved head, wearing a gray sweat suit, was already yanking my door open.

"Tweedle Dee!" he said, with a happy, booming voice. He slid in next to me while I scooted to the seat behind the driver. He slammed his door shut.

"My name is Cindy," the driver said. "Take it easy with the door, Darrel Day."

Darrel Day smelled like he'd just put out a small chemical fire. "I always take it easy."

"Where're you going?" Cindy said.

"I'm going with you, Tweedle Dee—you and this guy." He poked my shoulder. "What's up?"

"Don't call me Tweedle Dee," Cindy said.

"Fuck it, lady: just take me down to the harbor for a swim."

"There isn't any harbor. This cab only goes to real places."

We sat there in the cab on the corner. The heat sat with us. At least when we were moving, the air blew in my face and slowed down the sweating, but now all I could feel were my clothes sticking to my skin and my egg sandwich anchored in my stomach.

"Fuck it," Darrel Day said, "just take me where this guy's going." He nudged me. "Where're you going?"

I wasn't sure how to speak to this young man.

"He's going to the pet store."

"You gonna buy some animals and shit?"

"Um, no," I said. "My girlfriend? She has a cat."

"Come on," Cindy said. "What is this already?"

"Hold it," Darrel Day said, all serious. "Do they sell birds at the pet store?"

"I guess they do," I said. "Probably. But I wouldn't—"

"Then I'ma go to the pet store," Darrel Day said.

Cindy shook her head and accelerated into the right-hand turn. A warm breeze blew through the car.

"At the pet store I'ma get a tropical bird, Tweedle Dee."

"I've only been nice to you," Cindy said.

We passed rows and rows of bungalows separated by small plots of woods.

"I'ma get a big yellow bird that sits on my shoulder and hails your cab all day. I'll take one of those and . . . What else?" He tapped my shoulder. "Hey, what else should I get, man?"

"I don't know," I said, "a wooden leg?"

Darrel's laughter filled the car, his body rocked in his seat, and he gripped the headrest of the passenger seat in front of him with his large hands as though to steady himself against the force of his own jollity. "Yeah! Yeah! A leg and a bird and a—and a . . . a hook! Yeah! I'll be Pirate of the Harbor, hijack cabs all day! And guess what my bird's gonna say. Guess. He's gonna say, 'Tweedle Dee!'" He raised his voice and pursed his lips. "'Tweedle Dee!'"

"Up yours, Darrel Day," Cindy said. "Okay?" A bunch of blocks ahead of us, the light on William Floyd Parkway turned from green to red.

"Aw, shucks," Darrel Day shot back, "I'm just joshing with ya, Tweedle."

Soon we were stopped at the light. The southbound lanes on the other side of the parkway were clogged to a halt with traffic.

"Where're all these cars going?" Darrel Day asked.

"To Fire Island," Cindy said. "Where else?"

"I wanna go to the beach, too."

"Well, this cab's going to the pet store."

"Fuck birds. I'ma go to the beach." He threw a crumpled dollar at the windshield, bolted out of the car, slammed the door shut, and jogged across the median to a cab idling between two SUVs.

Now there went a guy blown around by the wind of any idea that might've whispered in his ears. What a careless way to live, I thought, and scary, too, when seen from the outside.

"You okay?" Cindy said.

"Yeah. Are you okay?"

"I'll be fine."

About ten minutes later, we arrived at the pet store. There was a sporting-goods store in the same strip mall, and right then, as we pulled up, I thought of Rose's passion for volleyball and decided to get one for her. I went there first, and then to the pet store.

But is it my fault that, later, the cat had seizures? I'd say no. Cindy had me rushing in and out of those places, and that tripped me up.

"I'll be right back," I said.

"I can't wait here for an hour," Cindy said, in a way that made me think she probably would wait. She'd probably waited countless times before.

"Two minutes. I swear I'll be in and out." I kept my word.

See, I wasn't to blame, and I guess Cindy wasn't either, really, but if you want to point a finger, then point at the store clerk who didn't tell me there was a big difference between a flea dip for cats and a flea dip for large dogs. I thought flea dip was flea dip.

"You should've read the label," my neighbor in the red lifeguard shorts would later say. Yeah, him—the jogger—the guy who, while I was stuck on my cab ride, was being a wonderful neighbor to Rose by washing some of the fleas off the cat in a disposable baking pan of warm water and dish soap suds. Rose stood by with a towel. They were drinking cold beers the man had brought over. What else they did, I don't know. By the time I got home, he was rinsing the soap off the cat.

"Look, you got a ball," Rose said to me.

"Who's this?" I said.

"He lives down the block. His uncle used to be an animal doctor."

"I know a thing or two," the man said. "Ain't that right, Mr. Cat?" He held the cat in the air and it dripped like a sopped shirt. "*That's* a cat. That's a *good* cat." The man looked me up and down, patted dry his free hand on his shorts, and offered it for a shake. "I'm Ted. You must be Dan. Hey, Rosie, how about we give Dan a beer?"

Next thing I was dipping the cat, and Rose took Ted's beers out of my fridge and set them in a plastic bag full of ice—refreshments for the game of soccer Ted was setting up. He built a goal from milk crates and two-by-fours he found along the chain-link fence. With the cat in the shoe-box recovering from its dip, I joined the game as goalie, deflecting a few shots but mostly just watching Ted and Rose shuffle up and down the yard with the ball.

"It's all in the footwork," Ted said to Rose. Their legs bumped together, and they stepped on each other's toes, playing barefoot as she had only heels and he didn't want to hurt her with his sneakers. The whole thing was ridiculous, never mind our soccer ball was, in reality, a volleyball.

"Are you sure you can play all right in that dress?" I said.

"She's doing great," Ted said.

A flea bit my arm. I rubbed him out between my fingers. "I'd like to go to the beach," I said. "We should go swimming. I can buy you a bathing suit, Rose."

"I can't swim," Ted said. "I'll drown."

"Aren't you having fun here, Dan?" Rose said, trying to step into Ted's action.

"I'm having lots of fun." A few blocks away, an ice cream truck blared a catchy new xylophone tune. Children shrieked somewhere. Ted stared down Rose's dress while managing to keep the ball between them with a little give and take, ensuring no chance of anyone attempting a goal soon. My beer was empty. The sun had concentrated to a fiery nickel burning a hole in the sky. "Rosie," I said, "baby, I can read your mind. You want some ice cream. I can tell."

"What are you talking about?" she said.

That's when the cat flopped out of the box. "Look, he's moving."

They stopped kicking the ball. "What the?" Ted said.

Rose squinted at the cat. "Kitty?"

The cat stiffened except for the white tail slapping the ground.

"What the hell?" Ted said.

"Kitty! Psst!" Rose said. "Guys!"

I picked up the box, trapped the cat underneath, scooped him in, and clapped the lid shut.

Meanwhile, Ted started preaching to me. "Holy shit," he said, "what the Christ is this? There's a Saint Bernard on the flea dip bottle! This flea dip is for goddamn Bernards!"

Animal doctor Dr. Zenger, Ted's uncle, confirmed that yes, the flea dip was the culprit. His house was one of those rare nice ones raised up on stilts in case of flooding, where Ducky Lane curved with the shape of the bay, and in the distance Fire Island was a long line of sand holding a crest of ocean against the blue sky. He was the kind of dry-lipped, slender, gray-haired man you just didn't see much of anymore, aged but full to the skin with life. Although he was retired, Zenger answered his door wearing a green lab-coat-looking thing over a suit. The coat was splotched and smeared with what looked like fake blood and mustard.

"Ted?" Dr. Zenger said. "What are you doing here? This is a surprise. I'm surprised."

We told him about the cat, and after considering the situation, he let us in. The inside of his house smelled like paint and felt like a fridge. His bathroom was the size of my bungalow, with a root-beer-brown Jacuzzi, the same color as the towels.

On the counter by the seashell sink, Dr. Zenger opened the box and said, "My, he's a little thing. Yes, a male."

"That's what me and Rose thought," I said. "Rose and I."

Rose, standing as far away from me as possible in that huddle by the counter, continued ignoring me. She kept her eyes on the cat. "He looks cold, Doctor Zenger."

"That's because he's going through some kind of aftermath," Ted said. "It's giving him the shivers."

Dr. Zenger looked at his nephew for a moment and sort of smiled like he remembered a joke he didn't want to share with the rest of us. Then he looked at me. "You, scruff the cat."

"What should I scruff him with?"

Dr. Z. grabbed the back of the cat's neck and lifted it out of the box. Kitty went limp. "Like this," Dr. Zenger said, "with your hand. Scruff the cat with your hand. Hold him here, like this, over the sink." He put the cat back in the box and it spasmed again.

I grabbed the cat behind his neck, lifted him, and once more he went limp.

"What should I do?" Ted said.

"Go to the living room," Dr. Zenger began. "Collect my paintbrushes and rinse them thoroughly in the kitchen sink."

"But I want to help with the cat."

"You are helping. I happen to be in the middle of a seascape. If that paint dries on my brushes, you'll be paying extra for this."

When Ted left, Dr. Zenger turned to Rose and said, "Go to the hall closet, second door on the right. Find a bottle marked 'Oxydex Shampoo' on the third shelf. On the fifth shelf find a bottle marked 'diazepam'—"

"Valium," Rose said, sure of herself.

"Find the diazepam next to the ketamine."

"K," Rose said.

"It's hard to find, actually," the doctor said. "I'll get it."

"This thing'll be washed three times today," I said.

Rose stared at me, then looked at the fish tank above the toilet.

"Would you like to have a bathroom like this?" I said.

"How does anybody come to be like you?" Rose said.

"What did I even do, Rose? Why don't you just admit what your problem is?"

"My problem?" she said. "What, is this about Ted? He was being a helpful neighbor. I'm talking about the picture of the dog on the flea dip. You were against the cat from the start. If it wasn't for Ted—"

"I knew it," I said. "I knew it was Ted."

"You're not even my boyfriend," she said, "and you're acting stupid."

I knew I wasn't her boyfriend—I'd only known her for eighteen hours—and, yes, maybe I was jealous; maybe I had a picture of us, in my mind, stretching out past that day, past the beach and into the next morning, she and I suntanned and in my bed, and even the cat licking our toes trying to wake us up, and maybe all this fantasizing had to do with the way a wedding could make a guy think about his bachelor existence, about how a woman could make him want to stop rolling blindly through life so, when he was old, he wouldn't feel like something the wind picked up and blew across town and back again every day. She'd make my life like a furnished house, and we'd watch the sunset from the porch I'd build. So yes, I was jealous. But stupid?

"I wouldn't want to be your stupid boyfriend."

"I wouldn't ask you anyway. I'm done with you. You're all used up."

"Why don't you go ask Ted? I'm sure he qualifies for stupid boyfriend."

"Maybe I'll marry him."

"Good."

"Good."

"You can have the ball."

"I don't want it."

"Good. I'll keep it."

All told, fixing the cat cost me twice what I spent a week on lotto, and that included the "take home" discount Dr.

Zenger gave me, which meant I was responsible for disconnecting the little plastic bag of fluid attached to the cat. I also had to feed him these tiny Valiums every four hours until sometime the following afternoon while trying to get the little sucker to eat. Dr. Zenger assured me, glancing at Rose—who didn't look happy at all, the way she stared at those orange fish in the tank—that the Valium was only two milligrams, and though the pills were fit for human consumption, it would take a handful of them for one of us, hypothetically, to feel anything, leaving nothing for the cat, which would be a very bad thing. He trusted we'd act responsibly.

"I'll be very responsible," I said. "This little guy is safe in my hands. Ain't that right, Mr. Cat?"

The bay looked nothing like Dr. Zenger's seascape painting, which he'd made us all behold before we left.

"You don't even want her!" Rose barked.

"Hand it over!" Ted said.

"No," I said. "I paid for it. I'll do what I want with it."

"Oh, God," Rose said, "he's gonna hurt the cat!"

"If you hurt that cat," Ted said. "You fucking hurt it—"

"You'll give me a taste of your aftermath?"

I wasn't even facing him. That's how cheap the shove was. As I fell forward I managed to set the box on the street and steady my footing. I turned and went after him, tried to scruff him around the neck but he side-stepped, turned behind me, and hugged my waist in an attempt to launch me over his shoulder. Luckily, I got a good hold of his leg, which was pretty solid timber, and managed to slip enough through his grip to right myself. We mostly twisted in each other's arms after that, and Rose wedged her hands in there between us, trying to pry us apart.

"Stop!" Rose said.

"Get the cat!" Ted said. "Get the cat, Rose! Run!"

"Touch my cat. I dare you."

A flea crawled into my eye and Ted got me in a reverse choke hold with my face toward the ground, the kind of move wrestlers use before they power-drive their opponents. Just then, Dr. Dick Zenger came onto his balcony in the sky. "Ted! Leave those people alone!"

"He started it!" Ted shouted back.

"Not in my neighborhood!" Dr. Zenger said. "Do I have to call your mother again?"

We broke apart, the two of us standing there looking like runners who'd just crossed the finish line. There was no clear winner.

"Come on, Rose," Ted said. "Get the cat."

"No," Rose said, her voice shaken. "We'll get our own cat."

Ted's panting mouth formed into a smile. He gave me the finger. Rose grabbed his hand and pulled him away. In a few steps they locked their fingers together. Ted looked back, smirking. About a block away, Rose stopped and put her hands under her dress and rolled the garter down her leg.

Then she held the garter out like a used tissue and dropped it to the ground.

I ate Rosie's egg sandwich that night, which didn't taste so bad cold. I also drank the rest of Ted's beer, and then I went to Handy Pantry for another six-pack and scratch-off. The third ticket won back the money I'd spent on the cat. When I returned from the store with the winnings, I found a joint that had been snubbed out on my steps. I'd already taken Lucky off the fluid bag, and he was coming down from the first dose of Valium. He could lift his head and maneuver a little. I offered a bit of egg white from my fingertip and he licked it into his mouth. He tried to walk. In half a step, he tumbled to the side and lay there, next to where I sat on the floor in the kitchen area, and we listened to the weekend sirens growing outside in the moonlight. Then Lucky turned his white face to me, quietly purring a proud, rolling purr. He was getting his self back. In a day he'd be on his feet, sniffing around the bungalow and passing the time with a balled-up sock. In two days, he'd stretch out on the windowsill to overlook his domain. Then he'd sneak outside, slip under the fence by the woods, and disappear into the wilds of Floyd Harbor.

But on the day before the cat left, I saw Ted. He was wearing the same shorts, this time with a T-shirt. He was sitting out on my porch in the rain.

I opened my door. "What's going on?"

"Oh, sorry," he said, "I don't mean to intrude, but I think I left something here on your steps."

"I haven't seen anything."

His cockiness was gone, and his shoulders were hunched.

"How's Rosie?" I asked.

"I don't really know. I think she went back to where she came from. Where is Rose from anyways?"

"No idea."

He put his hands on his hips and looked out to the road. "So, Dan, I was just thinking right now: how about you and me grabbing one of those beers, you know, from before?"

"I drank those beers."

"Oh," he said. "Hey, did you hear about the guy they arrested at the gas station yesterday? They say he took a whole sheet of acid."

"I don't really have time for small talk. I have to go to work soon." I had plans to pick up the Monday classifieds, see what was on offer.

"Yeah, I've got some things to do too. So, then, I guess if you see Rosie again, just tell her 'hi' from Teddy."

"Sure thing."

Back inside the bungalow, the bouquet of yellow flowers Rose had caught at the wedding lay dying on top of my radio. After some consideration, I put them in a thermos with water. It didn't look right, those flowers on the windowsill with their petals opened like mouths trying to suck up whatever sunlight was coming through the clouds, clinging hopefully to their little lives. The cat was on the sill, too.

He dismissed the bouquet and brought his attention to the world outside. Summer was almost over. The leaves were starting to turn. Soon they'd fall like loose change from the trees.

Battle of Floyd Harbor

My father decided to go back to the war. We thought it was a phase, like that year he went around at night posting signs on telephone poles that read, WHERE'S THE HARBOR? But this wasn't a phase. One of my brothers spotted him polishing his boots in the basement, whistling a familiar marching tune. Dad had set up base down there after losing his job as a cockpit mechanic on F-14 Tomcats. The Cold War had ended and, slowly but surely, the United States didn't need so many fighter jets anymore. My oldest brother tried telling my father that the Vietnam War had also ended, many years ago, and that there was no way he could go back. But my father just said, "*Baloney*." Then he sent my brother upstairs and locked the door.

"He said 'baloney'?" Seth said.

"He also said I was full of shit," Alex said. "And he was hooking up a private telephone line."

We knocked on the floor and called his name. Dad pretended he wasn't there.

"What's his number?" Mom had us all lined up, pointing a comb at us that she used for untangling her curls.

"I don't know," I said. The others said the same. None of us had our father's number.

"I'd give it to you," Darrel Day said. "We all would if we had it."

"Maybe you should call information," said Tim. He was the logical one.

"Good. Any other ideas, Tim?"

Soon all ten of us children had our heads to the kitchen floor and listened for his phone to ring. Our baby sister thought we were playing a game. She laughed and drooled. She slapped the floor with her palms and yelled some nonsense at the linoleum.

"Hello?" Dad said when he picked up.

"I wish we could've talked about this." Mom stood over us, floorboards creaking with her steps, twisting the phone cord around her finger.

Beatrice cupped her hands to the floor. "Daddy!"

We shushed her. Our breathing was the only sound for a while.

"What do you want from me?"

"You need to get a job."

"I had one."

"You need a new job."

"I'm fighting a war here. Do you know war? How am I supposed to do both?"

Mom always had an answer. "Split the day in half."

His next job was school security guard, sports field patrol, graveyard shift, weekend. District: Floyd Harbor. Division: High School. I awoke in the night from a dream and came to visit him. He was parked by the tennis courts. He crossed names off a list and tried to remember other names of men he fought alongside in the war. The best he could come up with were Boston, Tennessee, and Cleveland—the names of the places they were from. His security uniform was a chrome badge pinned to a light blue shirt tucked into dark blue slacks.

"You look professional," I told him. "Mom says she likes a man in uniform. That's why she fell in love with you."

"Uniforms," Dad said, turning his list over, scanning his notes. He took a sip of beer. He needed to get the platoon back together. I had heard about it through the wiretap. Well, not directly. I got it from Darrel Day, who'd got it from the brothers who made the wiretap, Tim and Sam.

"Dad said it was time to fight," Darrel Day had said, "and the other men said no way, I'm not going back, I have family to think of. Some of those men said they caught

Agent Orange. Maybe those Agent Orange guys joined with Dad already and they were talking in code."

"Darrel Day, what?" He was making me carry the two gallons of milk home from the store. It was part of my strength training. Darrel Day could've easily carried those gallons.

"He's going to the war," Darrel Day said. "Dad's going to war."

The patrol car windows were fogged with Dad's breath, the twelve-pack mostly empty, and he kept a bottle of garlic-and-herb salad dressing in the glove box. He told me a story about how he had escort duty at the end of his tour in Vietnam. He had to accompany a dead soldier from Da Nang to California, and then go through the funeral proceedings. The casket had to be kept closed. After the burial, the dead soldier's family wanted my father to stay with them and take their son's place in the family. He stayed with them for a week, sleeping in the dead soldier's bedroom, and they called him by the dead soldier's name.

"But what happened before that? You never told me what you went through in the war."

He looked at me for a long time. Then he looked through the windshield, and something only he could see in the distance held his gaze. Mom called this his ten-mile stare.

In the morning at home, Dad took a rock from the trunk of his car and rolled it into the yard to be with all the other rocks he'd collected over the years. He pulled a handful of

smaller stones from his pockets. Then he went to the basement and locked the door behind him.

There were thousands of rocks in our yard. No one knew
where he found those rocks, or why he collected them. Two
of my brothers worried themselves over it. What were the
rocks for?

"It's a puzzle," said my oldest brother, Alex. "It's a puzzle
about Dad."

Seth, my second-oldest brother, disagreed. "This is our
inheritance," he said. "We should take these stones and
build a house."

"That's practical," Alex said. "But our father's not a practical man. He's trying to tell us something."

Today, Alex and Seth had arranged the rocks by color.
They told our three teenage sisters to collect the small rocks.
The girls were already getting bored with the project, stay-
ing away from the piles for increasingly longer periods.

"Are you making any progress?" I asked.

Alex stopped pushing a tire-size boulder across the driveway. He caught his breath and stared at the piles. "There's
something to this. I can certainly feel it."

"I feel a knot in my back," Seth said. "But, yeah, I guess
it's starting to make some sense."

"Did you ask Dad if these rocks mean anything?"

They looked at each other. Then they looked at me as
though I'd asked the stupidest question in the world.

"Shut up. You're not doing anything. You're just scrib-
bling in that notebook."

I told them I was too tired to move stones. I'd been up for most of the night at the edge of Dad's war, pushing against it, trying to step inside. Also, I was hungover. The girls played quiet games along the edge of the property.

Midnight, moonlight, sports field: we watched as a naked body squirmed on top of another. It looked like a pale fish trying to swim across the grass.

Dad was supposed to shine a light on those lovers, maybe beep his horn—anything to make the couple scramble for their clothes and run for the fence. He was supposed to log this incident in the appropriate time slot on the top form of the clipboard. Instead, he finished his beer and cracked another open.

What did my mother think of our new situation? She had to pretend to be happy, at least at first. My father had obeyed her wish. He'd found a job, a small one tucked away in the sports field behind the high school, and in exchange he could spend his days in the trenches. She'd granted him that. Still, she'd forgotten about herself. How could they have any kind of meaningful relationship? Instead of sulking, though, my mother concentrated on the positive. The yard had never looked so good, she pointed out through the kitchen widow, with all the rocks organized by color one week, and then by shape the next week, and then by size the last week in June. Every evening the landscaping surprised her. "And since he's been working nights," she said, drying her hands on a dishtowel, "I have the bed to myself. That's not so bad. I like to stretch out."

But on top of my father's small salary of $240 per week before taxes, on top of his use of alcoholic beverages as a way of transporting himself back to the war, my mother was in danger of being lonely. She'd only just given up being pregnant and having babies, and only because she'd reached the age of fifty. Her tubes were on the verge of falling out. Her words. Having more babies was out of the question. In the mental plan book, that next phase was to have those tubes tied and take vacations around the world together, just Mom and Dad. Us older children could stay home and watch the babies for those few weeks out of the year. She would've happily settled for less than that. She didn't envy the luxuries the Joneses had, but where was her properly working dishwasher, or kitchen cabinets that weren't water-logged due to the leaky plumbing? The floors needed swab-bing every day. There were mouths to feed. We needed more money. All these things, except for mopping the floors, were the things my father used to handle.

"Report upstairs!" Mom said.

"I'm busy!" he said. Machine guns ratta-tatted.

"We need more money!"

"I'm changing my number. It won't be listed this time." He hung up.

It was becoming clear to Mom that her only option was

to put on her best clothes, strap baby Erin to her back, and get a job at the animal hospital.

Another thing I learned from those nights I kept Dad company at his job was that mouthwash is too obvious a cover for alcohol breath. That's why Dad gargled with salad dressing after his shift. But his supervisor was a retired detective who had trained his senses to pick up the smell of cat fart carried in a breeze from two miles away. He didn't have to work too hard to catch on to Dad. The security department took back the patrol car keys and walkie-talkie. The badge was his own. They might have called the police on him for driving the patrol drunk across the field, but the police were busy that morning with an incident at the USA gas station involving a naked guy who had taken too much acid. Dad walked home and crept back into the basement.

My sister Tara started passing the time modeling her bathing suit in the bathroom mirror. Mom split her time between her job with the animals and another one with retarded adults. She'd come home, put a new cat on the floor, and then bang on the basement door.

"Seventeen hours I worked today," she'd say. "I suppose you've drank as many beers."

"I don't think he's home," Tim said from his station at the kitchen table. He took the headphones off. "There hasn't been any sound."

"I heard a sound," Erica said. She was on her knees, swabbing the floor.

"No, you didn't," Tim said.

"I did."

"No."

Mom said, "Ba— Bea— Erica and Tom . . . Tim. Stop arguing. Hey, you, how do you think he is?"

"What?" I said. "I don't even know what you guys are talking about."

"We're talking about Dad. Is he home? You talk to him sometimes. What do you think?"

"What do I really think? Well, some of us think he's in battle. Like, right now."

During that period, my brothers and I passed some weeks watching little Beatrice and rearranging rocks. During that period, Tara, finally bored of looking at herself and yearning for the attention of structured parental supervision, decided to go out and find boys for sex. I can't fathom where my sister met these boys. I can't see them eating ice cream on the beach or roller-skating or sitting down to dinner with their families. Like I said, I was paying attention to Beatrice. I was playing with rocks with my brothers, trying to figure out Dad. Because Tara became pregnant, I can only imagine Tara and the boy as fish trying to swim across the high school sports field at night, all force and no grace, the promise far surpassing the act.

Cats my mother brought home multiplied, most of them missing ears or blind in one eye, and then small dogs appeared, suffering the same deformities. Mom herself had lost some teeth, and there was nothing to do about it since the dental coverage had expired. She slept with her menagerie on the bed in her room. They shed on her clothes. They shat and pissed on the floor. But surrounded by their warm bodies, sleeping, Mom looked happy.

Darrel Day asked if I wanted to join a gang.

"I don't know?"

"Fool!" he said. And he flicked my forehead.

"Dick."

He was much bigger than me even though we were about the same age, but he wouldn't seriously hurt me. He'd played football for varsity the first year of high school. I never played sports. People at school asked if we were really brothers. And if we were brothers, why was Darrel Day black?

"Never join a gang," Darrel Day said. We had been walking by the bay and ended up at the burned-down Bayview Hospital. I don't know when he started smoking menthol cigarettes.

"Are you in a gang?" I had been meaning to ask him.

"You ever heard of the Starter Posse?" Darrel Day said.

"No."

"Then just forget it." He sucked on the cigarette and blew out cough-drop smoke.

Soon, a sedan pulled down the gravel pathway hiding in the tall grass. The nose met us at the front of the clinic. "It's my friend Grady," Darrel said. "He's cool."

We got in the backseat of Grady's car.

"Is this your man?" Grady said, reversing out of the grass.

"He's good," Darrel Day said.

"Hey, Little D," Grady said. "You ever do lookout before?"

I didn't know I was Little D. There wasn't a D in my name. Later, I learned Grady liked to give out nicknames.

"What's lookout?"

"Exactly," Grady said. "What's that? What's lookout?" And then he laughed.

One thing was for sure: Grady was no cat burglar. Darrel Day and Grady kicked the front door in and smashed everything breakable as they went room-to-room while I waited at the edge of the woods for the police or neighbors to show up, at which time I was to let out a whistle. But Grady and Darrel Day were out of the Joneses' house before the police came. We only heard their sirens later, when just Darrel Day and I walked through the woods back home. We came upon a boat, parked behind the shed, in the shade where the trees had stepped out into the yard. The boat might have been there for a while before we noticed it. It was docked on a trailer. Then we saw a rowboat by the cord of firewood. Report the next morning included an eyewitness account of the arrival of a third boat, in which a truck backed the trailer down the driveway, unhitched it, and quietly drove off in the dawn.

"Does anyone know where the boats are coming from?" said Helen. She was always asking questions like that, but we didn't usually listen to her. "Maybe they're coming from the same place the extra money's coming from."

"What money?" Alex said. "There's no extra money."

"Mom found some money under her pillow last night," Helen said.

"The tooth fairy," Darrel said. We all laughed. When Darrel Day came to us from the inner city to spend the summer in the country, way back when we were five, he suggested we catch some jellyfish to put on peanut butter sandwiches. Darrel Day had a strange way of seeing things.

After a time, especially when they'd been moved around, it was hard to keep track of just how many boats there were. The number kept changing. Every time I came home, my tally was wrong. Boats are no different from animals or children.

Outside my window, my five-year-old sister, Beatrice, was making a giant man on the ground out of whatever stones she could carry. There was no joy in the way she lined them up to make his elbow bend.

"Whatcha doing?" I said.

She looked up at me, leaning out my window. "Where's Tara?"

Tara was a phantom flitting past doorways, disappearing around a closing gate. In a few months, she'd cup her arms under her bulging belly the way my brothers carried stones. Seth and Tim had started using the stones to build a house of their own on the edge of the property. My mother and Erin, her baby, seemed attached to each other, spawning deformed animals that would slink away into the woodwork. When we opened the pantry for cereal for little Beatrice's breakfast, a white cat with yellow eyes we'd named Spooky would leap out and take off running.

Beatrice and I spent the rest of the day making a woman, making children, making babies out of the dwindling pile of stones. Then we made a flat stone house. We laughed at the jagged teeth in the stone people's mouths as the sun went down. She liked seeing the stones that way. We fell asleep together on the couch, and when I woke up deep in the night, I was wet. She'd peed on me.

I heard voices outside. Six men sat around a campfire ringed with stones on the shore of the forest, and they all wore paper slippers and blue pajamas from the veteran hospital. Dad sat among them in his security uniform. Their words went off like bombs. After sunrise, they organized on a mission to get more beer.

"We need our bravest men," Dad said.

I listened through the hole in the kitchen wall, where the pipe for the broken dishwasher used to snake through to drain into a bed of rocks outside. Good thing the dishwasher had puttered out a few days earlier. It would not

shut off one day and it flooded the floor in soapy water.
My brothers and I had spent hours on our hands and
knees sopping up what we could with a mop and old rags.
I was going to take the busted machine to the scrapyard
for more cash, but we had no car to get it there because,
we figured out, Dad had traded his Datsun for that first
fishing boat. That's where the S.S. *Calenture* had come
from.

Bums we'd seen lurking behind the convenience store now
lived in the other boats with the veterans. Or maybe all
of them were veterans, and some of them were homeless
before this fleet gathered. Now they were all first mates.
By morning, their beer cans lay crumpled around the yard.
Beatrice and I collected the cans in plastic shopping bags
and took them to Handy Pantry to cash in.

Walking home from Handy Pantry, we saw a sign on a
telephone pole that read: WHERE'S THE HARBOR?

"There's no harbor in Floyd Harbor," I said, smoking
thoughtfully.

"What's a harbor?" Beatrice said. A bit of popcorn flew
from her mouth.

"It's a place where you park boats." We walked on. I
could smell the ocean. Burger wrappers collected sand along
the side of the road. "What do you think of this place?"

"What place?"

"This place where we live."

"Too many people drink here," Beatrice said. "And they all live in our backyard."

We took the scenic route home, past the bay, and we saw that our town was sinking. The roads five blocks inland were flooded. An old man in a doctor's coat stood in water up to his knees on the corner of Ducky Lane and Dogwood Drive with a canvas on an easel, painting the orange horizon. A gang of children ran around the corner, kicking their legs up, splashing one another. A pimply boy rowed a dinghy down Bayview Drive. Tara was in that boat.

"I fucking hate rowing," the boy said to her.

I called her name, but she didn't hear me.

At home, our father stood illuminated by the refrigerator light. He was thin. He slapped a piece of meat on a piece of bread. He closed the fridge and slipped out the back door. A white cat slipped inside. My sister and I went to the window and watched our dad sidestep a man on the ground, empty bottle in hand. Others milled around, scratching themselves, huddled in groups like conspirators, some roasting what looked like small, wild game over the fire pit. Our dad climbed into his boat and ate half of his sandwich. Chewing and swallowing, he looked to the window where we stood before he entered the cabin and closed the door.

The end of the world we knew was coming—it was beginning to disappear. My father had foreseen it. That night, the floods came. The winds carried his boat out to sea. And that was the last we ever saw of him.

Stacked Mattresses

‖‖

On the weekend before the flood, I awoke to Grady sitting in my wheelchair. He was watching the Shopping Channel, which accounted for the charismatic man showing up late in my dream, trying to sell me a watch that was a cross between the watch I owned and a watch I wanted. I found my glasses in the couch cushions, put them on, and propped myself up.

In a suit, clean-shaven, his hair tidy, Grady had acquired a squarish appearance. "You probably need some coffee," he said. "Milk, no sugar, how you like it."

Two take-out cups steamed on the coffee table. The room was warm. Grady must have mixed up my remotes when he turned the television on, and shut off the AC by mistake.

I took the remote from the table and switched the AC back on. "Grady, what's happening?"

"You're just not going to believe it," he said. With his thumb, subtly, he rolled a gold band on his ring finger.

"You got married?" I said.

"That?" he said. "Oh, yeah, she's a real princess. I want you to meet her."

I couldn't guess who Grady had married. Most of the women he dated were mythological to me, his relationships too ephemeral to include introductions to friends. Or the relationship only existed as a plan in his mind. The last infatuation was with a redheaded beauty—they were all beauties—in a tumultuous relationship from which Grady was attempting to rescue her. I had wished him luck, then he'd continued his quest into the rain, his sweater's hood drawn tight to his head. He'd slipped through the gate and disappeared up the street.

"Is she someone new?" I said. "So fast?"

"You have to take your opportunity," Grady said. He touched the knot of his tie as though to make sure it was still there. He grinned, expecting me to say something more.

"We should have cake," I said. "I have birthday cake in the fridge. It was my birthday two days ago."

"Hey, I didn't know you had a birthday." Grady got up and went into the kitchen area. "Wow, happy birthday! I would have come around if I knew. Congratulations." He took the cake from the fridge. "Chocolate!"

"But you just got married," I said. "You must have been busy."

"I got married two months ago," Grady said. "Wow, has it been longer than that since I last saw you?" He found a knife in the drainboard, and then outlined his plan for two slices in the frosting. His movements were calculated.

I sipped my coffee. The AC's cool breeze washed over me. Grady sank the blade into the cake. I might have told him that in the time between this meeting and the last, I went on a date myself. It was a blind date. She made no mention of my disability. Her smile never faded. She made constant eye contact. I called her up a few days later. I left a message on her machine. Then I found out she had met someone else.

"A day mother from the home baked that cake," I said.

"Really? One of the mothers?"

"She remembers everyone's birthday."

"That's real nice. Did she bring the cake here, to the house?"

"No, no, she gave it to me at work."

Now he smiled at me in the usual Grady way, a conspirator, a schemer, a believer in whatever he was thinking, and in that moment his suit looked to me like a party costume. It was beige with linen-white stripes, loose fit, like a paper shopping bag holding a single economy-size box of Lucky Charms. "She gave it to you at work?"

"It's just a cake," I said. "I swear." If Grady wasn't just married, why the suit?

Still holding the smile, he said, "Well, good news all around. Happy birthday cake to you, happy-ever-after to me." He licked the frosting off the side of the knife.

The cake was heavy and dry. The frosting on Grady's slice was thicker than the frosting on mine. As we ate, I wondered how he had gotten inside my house. I lock the doors when I'm home, and the windows stay locked because of the AC. I don't need to open them. But there was no point in bringing this up now. I had already made Grady feel welcome and accepted the coffee he brought. I had probably forgotten to lock the door. It happens sometimes.

"So, tell me about this woman," I said. "Your wife." And at the same time, Grady had begun to ask a favor.

"You can meet her," he said.

"What kind of favor?" I said. He still owed me a hundred and forty dollars from last time.

"A medium-size favor," he said. "It's for my job. I started a business. Did I tell you that?"

"Wow, congratulations again, Grady. What's the business?" Now the suit made sense.

"I'm a freelance distributor."

"A freelance distributor?"

"I work with the Cody Corporation. I exchange high-end goods between locations. It's a niche in the delivery sector. But my partner with the van, he moved on without notice, and I got all these mattresses to shift around. I'm a bit stuck, and it's kind of a make-or-break weekend for me."

"You're moving mattresses around in a van? I don't get it. Distribution?"

"Come around with me and I'll show you," he said. "It's straightforward. I get the mattresses, put them in the van, and then take them to another Cody store."

"Oh, you're getting them from the store, and then taking them to another store? I thought something else."

"What did you think?" Grady said. Then, as though the coffee was starting to work on him, he got it. "You thought they were stolen? Ha, that's a laugh! You were thinking I'm dealing with stolen mattresses from Cody's? No, it's all above ground. I go in the front door, get the merchandise, go out the front door. Working hours. Jeez, I don't know what you think of me sometimes."

"I thought you were a landscaper," I said. "You said you had all that equipment, and you were going in on it with some other guy."

"I moved on from landscaping. This is my new venture. But as I was saying, it's all make-or-break now. Without my van guy, I'm stuck."

Now I understood Grady's insistence that I see his new business in action. He needed my minibus.

"We'll make a day of it," Grady said. "I'll give you gas money. We'll go to lunch. You'll meet my princess later. What do you say?"

It was hard to say no to Grady. When I first came to Floyd Harbor back in high school, after my grandmother died and I moved in with my aunt, Grady was the first friend I had. Our English teacher, Mr. Luzzi, had assigned Grady the role of being my buddy and told Grady to look after me. At first, I thought Luzzi was pitying me because of my handicap, and I hated that, but soon I understood that Luzzi had paired us up for Grady's benefit. He had no friends. He talked too much, lied all the time, and he wasn't very smart. Other kids could trick him into doing stupid shit. That's how he ended up in the alternative program. In the parking lot, another kid had dared him to throw a rock into the open second-floor window of the science lab. The rock smashed into a glass case full of expensive flasks and beakers. The district put me in alternative because, up to that point, I had been homeschooled by my grandmother, and the entrance test pointed out big holes in my education. Within half a year, I was cleared, but I'd wheel over from the regular part of the high school to the alternative rooms during lunch because I was tutoring Grady in algebra and grammar. Whether I wanted to be or not, I had been partly responsible for Grady since then.

My glasses fogged when I rolled onto the ramp. The heatwave that knocked the power out a few days earlier would reach a peak today, according to the Weather Channel. Already breaking a sweat, I instructed Grady on removing the rows of passenger seats from the minibus. I had him bring them around to the side of the cottage where they'd be the least conspicuous. It was only after my driver seat docked and Grady was sitting in the passenger seat with a briefcase on his lap that I noticed the motorbike parked outside the fence. "What's that doing there?"

"That's mine. Pretty sweet, huh? I got that with my first earnings. It's a classic. It really needs to be in the shop getting worked on, though."

"You should put your next money toward a van," I said.

"Live and learn," Grady said. "I'll tell you what. You can hold on to the bike until I pay back the money I owe. I hope you don't think I forgot about that."

"When you have it," I said. What would I do with a motorbike?

Our first stop was the Cody's in North Harbor. Grady put his suit jacket back on, went in, and about half an hour later he came out with a mattress, helped along by a Cody's employee. They loaded the mattress into my bus and went back for a second mattress. Then we went to the Riverhead store, Grady singing the words he knew to "Hotel California" along with the radio.

At Riverhead, I waited again. Even without those backseats, the interior still held the smell of the clients from the home, like warm oatmeal, detergent, and a whiff of pee. But it was so hot outside I kept the windows rolled up and the AC on blast. I watched in the rearview mirror as Grady and the Riverhead Cody's employee jammed another plastic-wrapped mattress alongside the other two. Then they went back for the fourth mattress. When we left, the back of the minibus was full of mattresses.

"That guy was acting funny," Grady said. He took his suit jacket off. Sweat patches spread out from his chest and under his arms. "You shouldn't park in handicap on the next pickup. Park in the back of the parking lot, okay? This isn't a standard delivery vehicle. I have to make a good impression."

"What are you worried about?"

"It's just a little stressful sometimes," Grady said. "I have to look professional. I don't need them to see how I'm operating. Do you mind if I smoke in here?" He lit a cigarette.

"Grady, he's just the stock boy. Why would you worry about what he thinks?"

"He's not the only factor," Grady said. "I got a lot riding on this business."

I rolled his window down from the driver's side control panel. I usually wouldn't let anyone smoke in the bus, but he looked like he needed it. It looked like Grady had taken on more responsibility than he could handle.

We headed to Bellport for another pair of mattresses. Grady planned to tie them to the roof with rope he'd brought along in his briefcase. I didn't see how that was going to work, because my chair stowage took up the front half of the roof. The stowage slides open, the folded chair slides out on an aluminum frame, angles vertically, and is lowered on a steel bar attached to a pair of roll-down chains. I said the stowage would be in the way, but Grady told me not to worry, the mattresses weren't going to fly off on the parkway on the way from Bellport to the Islip store. He'd done this before. At Islip, the first delivery on today's route, he'd unload the two mattresses from the roof first. Then we'd hit Amityville and Freeport before heading back to Floyd Harbor with the empty minibus, stopping at the diner to meet his wife, and then back home to return the seats to the bus.

"Could the weight of the mattresses break my chair lifter?" I said. "I don't think it's meant to support extra weight."

"Don't worry about that. These mattresses are light."

I took the exit for the Bellport Outlet Center. "Maybe I'm dumb. I don't get it. Why would Cody's want you to shuffle their stuff around like this?"

"Like I said, it's a matter of distribution," Grady said. "It's a matter too small for their own delivery department, so they outsource to an independent. I fill the space between the delivery department and customer service."

I still didn't understand what he was doing, or why the first two stops had taken so long. It seemed to me that all there was to do was go into the store, get the mattresses, and load the minibus. But maybe there were checklists to consult, forms to sign, managers to talk to. Bureaucracy could be a time eater.

Parked at the far end of the Bellport Cody's parking

lot in the scant shade of a nature patch, I was still trying to understand the logic of Grady's business when a police cruiser pulled up to the front of the store. Over the tops of shoppers' cars heating up in the sun, I watched the officers get out of the cruiser. They vanished through Cody's automatic doors.

One cop led Grady out in handcuffs. The other carried his briefcase. I suddenly understood why he wanted me to park so far away, why he was afraid of the alert stock boy in Riverhead. I didn't know what crime he had been committing, but my minibus was full of evidence. I was an accomplice. The arresting officer guided Grady to the police car door, and Grady looked straight ahead. He looked ahead as he was helped into the backseat. The cop shut the door, the other one loaded the briefcase into the trunk, and then the officers turned their attention to the parking lot. Only then did Grady shoot me a look that was meant to tell me something. *Beware* seems appropriate. I gave him my best look to communicate fear and confusion, the look I already wore. He faced forward again and did not look back to me. I was on my own. One officer talked into her radio and waited by the car while her partner peered into the window of a white van parked in the second row. There was some gesturing, and then a black man in the driver seat climbed out of the van. People with shopping carts who had seen Grady's arrest were talking to people who had just happened by the scene, the main attraction now the bulky police officer with one hand out in front of him, talking to the black man, the black man already showing his palms to the officer, his shoulders in a defensive shrug. He was a teenager, maybe. He was wearing those baggy hip-hop clothes.

Drivers entering and leaving the center changed their routes for a closer look. I skirted the bus around the edge of the lot. I took the east exit. Either the police didn't notice me leave, with all the rubbernecking going on, or the *Colonial Home Guardian* logo on the side of my minibus deflected their suspicions.

I drove the back roads to Floyd Harbor full of terror. There might have been witnesses or parking-lot security images. And how was I going to get the mattresses out of the bus? I couldn't ask anyone I knew for help, because if anyone saw me with four mattresses in my bus, they would wonder what the story was. What would I tell them?

My landlady, who lives next door, wouldn't let me off without a full and believable answer. And because she is well connected in this town, she was bound to hear any bit of gossip about what went down in the shopping center a few towns over.

In Floyd Harbor, I made an early left and parked in the back lot of the Sunrise Diner, at the edge of North Harbor's business district. I had to find this woman Grady had only called his princess. He had said she was beautiful. He had said a few times that we'd meet her for a meal at the diner when the job was over, so I could only hope that this was a prearranged date, that this was the diner he meant, and that at some hour soon she would be there, if she wasn't already waiting. As I said, this so-called job had been taking longer than expected.

In the diner, there were no outer benches at the front end of the two rows of booth seating. Both booths were empty. I parked at the one with the better view of the front door and ordered a coffee I didn't need. In the late lunch crowd, there were two women I might have summed up as beautiful. One was with an old man, cutting up his hamburger. The other woman worked in a bank, judging by the name tag with the bank logo and blue pantsuit. The bank closes at noon on Saturday. She'd been waiting for a while. I couldn't imagine this Ashley rushing from work to meet up with Grady, though. She would have seen right through him. Her purse started ringing. She took out a cellular phone, drew the antenna, and said hello. Still talking on the phone, she looked at me, and I realized I'd been staring.

I looked away. The waitress was filling my coffee again, and there was a menu in front of me. I didn't want more coffee. I couldn't eat any of the food pictured in the pages of the menu. I'd had too big a helping of anxiety and cake for breakfast.

"Do you want to order anything else?" the waitress said. "Some food?'

"Do you have spring water?"

"Will table water work for you?"

"Table water's fine," I said.

"Are you waiting for someone?"

"No," I said. "I'm just enjoying the scene in here." I was never too good at small talk, and the fear nudging at my ribs wasn't helping.

Her egg belly pushed against her apron strings. She was staring dead at me, head down, eyebrow raised, her hair tied in a loose ball on her head. Her name tag said PRINCESS.

"Your name is Princess?"

"No," she said. "The last waitress died and left this uniform to me. Where's Grady?"

"He was arrested." I said this using my face more than the volume of my voice to communicate.

"Arrested? Shit! He's an idiot," she said. "I told him this would happen."

"You know what he was up to?"

"I know who he's been hanging out with," she said. "I'm not talking about you. I don't even know you."

If she didn't know who I was, how had she known I was with Grady? "He left me stuck," I said. "I need help."

"So just the eggs, number three?" she said. She took the menu from me. Quieter, she said, "I'm off at five." She tucked the menu under her arm. "White toast, coffee refill, the bill. Coming up."

Somewhere in my blind spot, I could feel the Greek manager watching us.

———

There was a wait at the handicap stall in the diner bathroom. Some guy in a suit was in there. Not going to the bathroom, not masturbating, not reading. He just stood in there like he was in an elevator, waiting for the door to shut. Was he smacked up on drugs? Of course, this had to happen in the handicap stall. No one expects us to show up.

He became aware of me. "Oh, do you need to get in here?" he said. He stepped out and I wheeled in. When I finished and came out of the stall, the man was still in the bathroom, water running over his wringing hands, staring into the mirror, mouthing words to himself.

The wait in the bus for Princess to get off work gave me time to think of other places I could have parked. By the Dumpsters, I'd be better obscured but more suspect. Handicap parking would put me in front of the diner, in view of the busy intersection of Montauk and Floyd, but it was the most obvious place to go because a handicap-tagged vehicle with a chair stowage on top looks odd parked anywhere else. It was an hour-and-ten-minute struggle to decide to go with my second option. I inched the bus around the front of the diner, but before I could get to the spot, a Floyd Harbor police cruiser pulled up and parked diagonally across the handicap row. They were on business serious enough to exempt them from parking laws. I pulled into the nearest space and shut the engine.

I should have turned myself in, before, in the Bellport

parking lot. If I had just come out to the police with what was happening as I understood it up to that point, why wouldn't they believe me? I was also in a wheelchair. I'm not blind to my advantage here, the innocence a wheelchair can conjure. But I had knowingly left the scene of the crime. If I had to talk, the only story that would come to me is the one I'm telling now, the truth. But would they believe it?

The police got out of the cruiser. Closing the doors, they surveyed the area with a quick scan. Then they went into the diner.

There was shouting. The officers were shouting for someone to put their hands up where they could see them. I waited for Princess to be led out in cuffs, and for Princess to point out my bus for them with her chin. "Oh my god," a woman kept saying. "I can't believe you did this!" People were cheering and laughing. Music started playing from the jukebox, and a few minutes later, the police emerged with take-out containers, bantering like buddies out on the town. They drove off with a farewell burp of the siren. A little later, more people started pulling into the diner. Then Ashley, the bank woman, came out with the bathroom man, holding hands and leaning into each other, stopping to kiss, getting into separate cars, one car trailing the other out of the parking lot.

Princess came out at 6:20 in jeans and tank top, the strap of a large denim bag over her shoulder. The sun brought out the red highlights in her hair, now hanging free to her elbows. She stopped short on the way to the bus. Her face asked a question. Then she came around the passenger side and got in. "I just had déjà vu," she said. "Why?"

"I don't know."

"Something familiar," she said. She looked at the diner. She looked at my legs. "We didn't meet before," she said. "I would have remembered you. It's something else."

"How did you know I was with Grady?" I said.

"He told me about you."

"That I'm the guy in the wheelchair?"

"Yes. He said you're like family to him. But he said the same thing about Kitkat, so I don't know what to believe."

"Who's Kitkat? What happened with the police before? I thought you were getting arrested."

"Why would I get arrested? What were you guys doing today?"

"All I know is Grady asked me to help him with these mattresses. That's all I know."

Princess looked in the back of the bus. "Fucking Kitkat."

"Who's Kitkat?"

"Don't bullshit me," she said. "I have a sixth sense."

"I really don't know who you're talking about."

"Kitkat? The one doing all the mattresses? You better hope Kitkat was in on this with you."

"I have nothing to do with this," I said. "I have no idea what's going on. I swear to God."

"Well, if you don't get rid of these," Princess said, "no

one is going to believe you have nothing to do with it. Kit-kat won't believe you have nothing to do with it."

"I don't want anything to do with anyone called Kit-kat," I said. I was panicking. "God, what is Grady into? You have to help me get rid of these. I can't do this by myself. I don't know where to take them. I can't get them out of the bus by myself."

"This is what I'd get arrested for," Princess said. "Aiding and abetting. Christ."

"For helping me? I didn't do anything wrong."

"Yeah, if you keep saying that, someone might believe you. Wait, do you live on Pinewood?"

"No, I live on Diana."

"Alone? What number?"

"One forty-three"

"Okay, we'll go there."

"I don't want the mattresses there," I said. "I just want to get rid of them."

"Do you want to keep them in the bus until we figure out where to get rid of them? That's your other option. In the bus or in the house."

"Can't we just throw them away?"

"Okay. Maybe you want to get caught dumping them in the woods. Don't you think that would look more suspicious than bringing them into a house?"

I had no argument. I started the bus and backed out of the space.

"Stop a second," Princess said.

"Why?"

"I have to pee."

"Really? You just left the diner," I said.

"I have to pee all the time," she said.

I pulled into the handicap space. She went inside. For five minutes, I wondered what kind of car this Kitkat might drive. I imagined something black with a long trunk and tinted windows. I imagined a Datsun with tape on the fender. There were all kinds of cars in the diner parking lot. From this vantage point, I also had a full view of the infamous WELCOME TO FLOYD HARBOR sign. The story was that, back in the mid-eighties, members from the Historic Society and Property Owners Association formed a committee to change the Mastics and Shirley to Floyd Harbor. They were the Committee to Rename the Mastics and Shirley to Floyd Harbor. They argued that the only way to attract business and wealthier residents was to ditch the names Mastic, Mastic Beach, and Shirley, and all the negative connotations that went along with them. Another committee formed, also composed of Historic Society and Property Owners Association members, to oppose the change. They were the Committee Against Floyd Harbor, and their main argument was that there was no harbor to substantiate the name change, only the bay. Anthony Aussie, real estate developer on the Floyd Harbor team, said investors would build the harbor, the same investors he had lined up to develop a section of the pine barrens into an upscale gated community. The Committee Against Floyd Harbor then argued that they weren't really doing anything to improve anyone's condition if they planned to build a giant wall between the haves (of the gated community) and have-nots (everyone else). Public debates at Floyd High School and the Mastic Beach firehouse grew heated. Anthony Aussie poured fuel on the fire by erecting the Floyd Harbor sign in Shirley on the corner of William Floyd Parkway and Montauk Highway months before a vote took place, and people already started believing they lived in Floyd Harbor. They even put bumper stickers on their cars that said I LIVE IN FLOYD HARBOR. A few enterprising entrepreneurs opened shops and adopted the name Floyd Harbor. Floyd Harbor Flowers. Floyd Harbor Pet Supply. Floyd Harbor Pizza. The other half of the residents put bumper stickers on their cars that said WHERE'S DA HARBOR?

When the town voted, Floyd Harbor was victorious, three to one. The pine barrens came down. Foundations for the private community were laid. Then Anthony Aussie disappeared with the rest of the investors' money. His body was found somewhere in New Jersey.

Now the three towns are collectively Floyd Harbor, but the peninsula on the bay, where I live, is still known as Mastic Beach, because of the sign at the corner of William Floyd and Neighborhood Road that never came down, welcoming drivers to the Mastic Beach Business District.

———

When Princess came back to the bus, I drove up to the exit. "Which way should I take?"

"Just drive normal. The way you usually go." She took a cigarette from her bag and lit it.

I was going to ask her to open the window, but then she opened it a crack and flicked her cigarette out. "Just one puff. I'm supposed to quit for a while." She put a hand under the curve of her belly. Her egg belly was a baby. I should have figured that.

"Those assholes," she said. "They scared the shit out of everyone."

"Who?"

"The police," she said. "They were pretending to arrest a guy in the men's room. The officers busted into the bathroom shouting like all hell, and they put the guy in handcuffs. When they were walking him out, this woman shrieks because it's her boyfriend they arrested, and she didn't know he was in the bathroom. She'd been waiting for him to show up. Then the two cops and the man get down on their knees, and one of the cops holds out a box with an engagement ring and the other has the keys to the handcuffs, and the man says, 'Will you marry me, Ashley?' And she's just standing there shrieking, 'Oh my god! I can't believe you did this!'"

"You sound just like her. I heard her from the parking lot."

"Please," Princess said. She put another cigarette in her mouth. Then she took it out of her mouth and slid it back into the pack. She fiddled with her purple lighter. "Can you turn the radio on?" She switched it on herself. The station was playing the opening riff of "Hotel California." That song played two or three times a day in the summer.

I reached for the dial, but Princess told me not to touch it. This was Grady's song. So I just drove, and she listened and nodded. Traffic thickened farther south, probably backed up at the Smith Point Bridge to Fire Island. While I waited for the song to end so I could ask her about Kitkat, I wondered how we were going to move the mattresses from the bus. And the seats had to go back in before work on Monday. The song faded as we approached Mastic Beach, and then a call-in radio contest began. Princess turned the dial to an ice cream jingle.

I turned the radio off. "I need to know what Grady's got me into. I don't need this kind of trouble."

"If you really don't know what you're into, then maybe it's better you don't."

"Why?"

"Because if you do know, and you tell what you know, that means you're in on it. And if you're in on it, and Kitkat's not involved, you'll be wishing."

"Wishing what?"

"I don't know," she said. She looked at my legs, my special driving mechanism. "I don't know what Kitkat would do to you."

———

Meredith's car was home. Her two grandsons played on the bus seats along the side of the cottage. When I pulled into the driveway, the boys ran back to Meredith's yard, around the boat, and into the house, calling "Grandma!" the entire way. "He's here!"

"Great," I said. I shut the engine.

"What?"

"My landlady's going to have questions." Out of the house came Meredith, trailed by her two grandchildren, who split off to go back to the bus seats with a bag of cookies, the six-year-old leading the five-year-old.

"Meredith?" Princess said. "Meredith's your landlady? No way!"

"You know her?"

"I knew her before I was born."

Princess was already getting out of the bus to greet her. "Hi, Merry!"

"Hi! Who's that?" Meredith said, taking her glasses from her bunched-up curls.

"It's me."

"Oh, Anne! I didn't have my glasses on."

She called Princess *Anne*. They embraced at the invisible border of the properties. Meredith's house is on the east side of the block, I'm on the west side. There is no fence between us because, she said, the properties are married. I don't really know what that means.

"So, this is where you live?" Princess said.

"You haven't been here before?" Meredith said. "You were here before."

"It's funny you say that, because I get a feeling I was. You used to live on Robinwood."

"I moved houses when the boys moved out. My husband lives there now. How's your mother doing? Is she still working at the Sunrise Diner?"

"No," Princess said, "she left to work in a home for the mentally handicapped. I have her old job at the diner now. Well, for the next few months I do. Then we'll see."

"You're pregnant," Meredith said. She put a hand on Princess's belly, her other arm around her back. "You should have told me you were pregnant." The way Meredith felt around Princess's bulge reminded me of a guy I used to know who read braille.

Meanwhile, from the swiveled-out driver seat, I waited to meet my folded wheelchair as it lowered from the roof stowage.

"Oh, duh," Meredith said, "so that's how you know Michael. From your mother's job at the home."

"He's so sweet," Princess said. "He's helping me with some of my stuff."

I unloaded myself. It was becoming hard to follow what was happening here. Princess and Meredith knew each other, but I wasn't sure how well. And Princess was just going to let Meredith go on believing I worked with her mother? I didn't know any women from the home who used to work at the diner. Maybe Princess's mother worked at some other home.

"With the baby coming, I thought I'd move into a new place. I'm staying with a friend for now. Michael's going to hold on to my bed and a few other things for me until it's ready. My husband would handle this, but he has to be away for a while. Thank God for Michael and his bus."

"Beep! Beep!" shouted one of the boys on the other side of the house, and then the other boy let out a few beeps, too. They were playing a traffic game.

"Are those Bethany's kids?" Princess said. "I still feel so bad about what happened to her." She frowned.

"We all do," Meredith said. "We feel it every day."

I had never met Bethany. She died a few years before I moved to this side of Floyd Harbor. She had been a mom since she started high school, around the time her own mother disappeared, and Meredith became Bethany's foster parent. Then Meredith became foster grandparent to the two boys. Bethany died in the passenger seat of a white convertible when the driver, who was high on some array of pills, crashed it into a tree. The driver became paralyzed from the waist down. They say he got what he deserved. I had heard the story a few times from people at work. They talk about all the local tragedies.

A young man passed on a bicycle on Meredith's side of the block. The bandana on his head matched the red of the bike.

"So, what are you doing to get ready for the baby?" Meredith said. "Are you doing Lamaze?"

"Oh my god, are you still teaching?"

"I have a class beginning Monday at Saint Jude's. Upstairs in the Parish Center. Do you want me to sign you up?"

"For Monday? What time?"

"Five thirty."

"Oh wait. My husband is away. I told you that, right?"

"Michael can come."

"What?"

"Michael can come. He can be your Lamaze partner until your husband comes back."

They both looked at me.

"Upstairs?" I said.

"They have a lift," Meredith said. "You didn't know about the lift in the church? Have you never been in the church, Michael?"

"No, yes. I wasn't sure if you said upstairs or something else."

"So, think about Lamaze and tell me before you go."

"I will," Princess said, and they embraced once more. "It's so good to see you again."

Meredith went back to her house, to a ringing phone. The two boys were quiet, probably finishing off the cookies. The young man on the bicycle passed again, this time on my side of the block. This time, the bicycle was blue.

———

Princess opened the back of the van. The mattresses wouldn't budge. Grady had jammed them in to make them fit.

"We need help," Princess said. She walked out to the road. She looked left. She looked right. Where was help?

The two boys had moved onto the boat. The boat was another one of those vehicles Meredith's middle son, Sal, dropped off. Last time, it had been a yellow Caprice Classic he wanted to restore. Eventually, the Caprice disappeared. The boat had been sitting on the trailer for a year now. The two boys pretended to drive the boat. The bow pointed at the cottage.

"Iceberg!" the six-year-old shouted.

Then they were both shouting, pointing at my cottage: "Iceberg! Iceberg!"

And Princess was talking to the man on the blue bike. He had stopped a few pedals in front of her. I wheeled down the driveway.

The man was saying, "What are you paying?"

"I'll think about it," Princess said. "I don't know yet."

"What's the job?"

"Moving furniture," she said, standing there like she was casually smoking, only there was no cigarette in her hand.

The bicycle guy retied the red bandana on his head, shifted his stance. "How about that motorbike? I'll do it for the motorbike."

"Keep dreaming," she said. "I'll pay you what you're worth."

The kids were finished shouting "iceberg." They jumped from the boat to the grass and disappeared into the shade of Meredith's yard.

It was after eight by the time the mattresses were stacked in my living space. I had a narrow passage to the end of the couch that was also my bed. Another passage led to the bathroom. The young man, Jay-Jay, lay on the mattress stack, recovering from the struggle of moving them alone.

"Now the seats go back in," I said.

"That's later," Princess said. She gave a sideways look, indicating Jay-Jay's presence without Jay-Jay catching on. Jay-Jay looked straight up at the ceiling. He was younger than I first thought, not in his twenties but maybe sixteen or seventeen.

"Is this the bathroom?" Princess said. She moved aside the curtain behind her that was the bathroom door. Under the trickling she made, Jay-Jay let out a quiet snore. He had fallen asleep.

"I was bursting," Princess said when she came out. She looked at Jay-Jay. "Is that comfortable?" She footed the stack.

Jay-Jay opened his eyes. "When am I getting paid?"

"Tomorrow," she said. "We have to get some rest."

"You said this was a one-day job. Maybe I won't come back."

"Maybe I woulda given you the motorbike. You won't know if you don't come back."

He sat up. "Tomorrow. Right." He peeled his sweaty arms from the mattress plastic and left without shutting the door behind him. "I know where you live," he said.

When he was gone, I said, "Why aren't we putting the seats back in?"

"You work Monday, right?" she said. "That gives us a day to figure out the mattresses. After that, we'll put the seats back in."

"I just want to get this over with."

"Who's doing who a favor?" she said. "It's too late to do anything else today. All this sneaking around is exhausting." Her shoes were off. She lay on the stack, leaning back on one elbow, and scooped the underside of her belly with her hand. She let out a sigh. It was hard to tell her age. Seventeen or thirty-five. "Do you have water?"

"Do you want a ride home?" I said. I was worried what Meredith would say if she saw Princess leave the cottage in the morning.

"Great," she said. "Let's go."

"I can get you in the morning to finish this."

But I couldn't find my keys. I thought I'd put them on the bar nub. Princess helped look in the couch cushions, the door lock, under the coffee table: the usual places. She checked around the ramp and the driveway. She looked in the bus. My spare keys were hanging in the staff closet at work. "What if that boy took them?" I said. "He was riding two different bikes before. He's probably a thief."

"Look who's talking," she said. "And how would he know how to drive it? Wait. Maybe the keys are under the mattresses."

"Check," I said.

"I can't," she said. "They're heavy. I'm pregnant. Shit. We'll have to wait for Jay-Jay to look tomorrow."

"But he might not come back. I don't know if you can stay here. Meredith is going to talk. Maybe I can pay for your cab. Shit, I need those keys."

"I can pay for my own cab," she said. "But what are you going to do if the boy does come back and steals the bus? Wheel after him? I can run. I should stay here." She sat on the stack of mattresses. "Damn. I didn't see this as part of the plan. But don't worry. We'll find the keys tomorrow. It'll be fine." She dug around in her denim bag. Then she stopped. "I gotta quit smoking already."

The last time I shared a room with a woman was when I lived with my aunt Brooke, before she moved to North Carolina and got married. Before Brooke, I lived with my grandmother, who raised me after the accident. I was thinking about the two of them, how they had stopped talking to each other some time ago, and then my grandmother died, and Brooke came to me out of nowhere, full of guilt, and took me in. She became like my mother for a while, and when I graduated she invited me to move down to North Carolina with her. She said I could get a place with her. I didn't go, and then she met a man at church and they got married. He'd been married before and had grown kids. My aunt was older than him, but it was a first marriage for her. Her life was suddenly changing. She changed from working in a bingo hall, reading books about serial killers, and watching episodes of *21 Jump Street* she'd taped off the television, and became a wife and churchgoer, a mother and grandmother. She had five step-grandchildren. She told me in a Christmas card two years ago that God had transformed her, and her invitation for me to move on down was still valid. Thinking about what that might be like helped keep my mind off the trouble I was in.

The full moon burned in the window. Every so often, Princess would snort, throw her body to lie on her other side, kick her feet out of the blanket I gave her. The mattresses wobbled and crinkled with her movements. There were too many springs at play. I kept hearing sounds of the summer night and wondered if any of them were Jay-Jay snooping, or the landlady checking in. I heard cicadas. When I did fall asleep, briefly, I had a dream that I was in an elaborate prank Grady had staged for me. I was awoken by the rise of sirens. The sirens were coming down Mastic Road toward my neighborhood. Then they traveled west on Neighborhood Road, about two blocks from me. A man was shouting. Other shouts joined in—police and culprit negotiating. I imagined Jay-Jay, cornered, caught moving stolen bicycles across town in the cover of night.

Well into my breakfast of coffee and cake, Princess said, "There's a lump in these mattresses. I felt it all night." She propped up on her elbows. Her hair seemed fuller today, as though it had decided on being curlier. "I bet the keys are under these mattresses."

"That's impossible," I said. "You wouldn't feel that."

"You ever slept on a Cody's mattress?" she said, stepping straight for the bathroom. "Times that by four." She closed the curtain and peed. "These mattresses are the worst. I can see why people are always returning them to the store. Oh!"

"What?"

She finished peeing and came out from the curtain. "I just figured it out, duh. We should return them to the store. Duh! We should return them! That's so obvious!"

"No, that's crazy," I said.

"What better place to hide them?" she said. "No one would suspect it."

"I don't know what Grady was doing," I said, "but it had to do with these mattresses. I'm not bringing them back to the store. We just need to get rid of them. I should've gone straight to the police is what I should've done."

There was a knock at the door. Three raps, and then,

"Hello?" It was Meredith. Princess stepped back into the curtain.

"I'm here," I said.

"Michael, I wanted to ask you about those bus seats. Did you finish moving the furniture? Because the bus seats are still outside. Don't you need them in the van? I can ask my Sal to come help."

"Oh, no. Don't do that. It just got late, so we're going to finish today. Thanks, though."

"And I remember what I wanted to ask you yesterday," Meredith said. "Whose motorbike is by the gate?"

"Good morning, Merry," Princess said, sounding sleepier than she did when she first woke up. "That's my motorbike. Do you want me to move it?"

"Anne? You're not moving in, are you?"

"Oh, no. I'm not moving in. It's just temporary storage until the end of the month. I stayed last night because it got late."

Princess made a gesture to her throat that said I should cough something up.

"It's just a favor," I said.

"You can have people over, Michael," Meredith said. "I just like to know what's happening in my backyard. Did you hear sirens this morning?"

"Was that on Neighborhood?" I said.

"There was some commotion at the USA gas station," Meredith said. "Come by later, Anne. I have samples and baby clothes to start you off."

When Meredith was gone, Princess turned back to me and saw the cake I had left for her. Halfway through her first bite, she said, "We'll have to go to Grady's. All my things are there." She swallowed. "We have to make it look like we're moving stuff. Merry's watching us." She licked her teeth. "Why is this cake so dry?"

"It's been in the fridge," I said. "We have to find the keys. We have to figure out the mattresses."

"We already figured them out. And if she sees us moving stuff into the house, she won't notice when we put the mattresses back in the bus."

I was going to say we didn't agree on returning the mattresses to the store, but instead I said, "Is your real name Anne?"

"Anne's my nickname."

"Grady said that motorbike is his."

"He borrowed it from me."

There was another knock, then a jiggle of the doorknob. "Who is it?" I said.

"You guys owe me," Jay-Jay said into the door.

As Jay-Jay stood the mattresses against the wall, he told the story of the sirens. There had been a naked guy at the gas station, pacing around the pump, waving the nozzle like a pistol in his bloody bandaged hand, saying he needed to get back to the water. Police caught him and put his ankles and wrists in zip ties. He flopped around like a fish and broke out of them. The police had to catch him again. This time they used real cuffs on his wrists and his ankles. The guy was still flopping in the back of the cruiser when they drove off.

"Who told you this?" I said. The story was too outlandish.

"I saw it," Jay-Jay said. "I think the guy plays varsity basketball."

"It was a high school kid?"

Jay-Jay lifted the bottom mattress. The keys were underneath.

"See?" Princess said. "I told you I felt the keys."

"He was expelled," Jay-Jay said. "That's what I heard, anyway. I try to stay away from that nut house."

I started driving to Grady's place, but Princess told me I was going the wrong way. Grady had moved to North Harbor. I made a three-point turn.

Grady's new house was in an area that was woods a few years ago. Now it was a collection of ranch houses. The houses still had factory tape on the windows. A few driveways had been poured, blocked off with gates made of empty paint buckets and lumber scraps. No one seemed to live in these houses. Either the developers had run out of money, or the workers were off for the weekend. The last part of Princess Anne's directions had me circle around the same block twice before we stopped in front of a place that had part of a lawn puzzled together. The lawn squares had turned brown. The rest were stacked in towers alongside the curb.

"Grady lives here?"

"That was the plan," Princess said. She went around back and opened the front door from inside. She invited Jay-Jay in. They came out with two standing lamps, then the parts of a wooden table, and then six chairs with high carved backs. The set looked like it could have been from an estate sale on a street in a fancier town farther east. Princess said she inherited the set from her grandmother.

Then they brought out cardboard boxes, each the size of a box a microwave oven might be packed in, all taped shut. There were maybe thirty of them. Princess really had planned to move away from this disaster of a future with Grady. His latest stunt had settled it for her.

Things started to feel normal. We were moving furniture. I was doing a favor for a friend, and she had hired a kid to help. Meredith's car wasn't in her driveway when we got back. Princess had Jay-Jay unload the table, chairs, lamps, and boxes into the cottage, bringing a mattress out between each trip and lining them up alongside the driver's side of the bus.

Jay-Jay wanted to know why we were putting the mattresses back in the bus. Princess explained that they were uncomfortable and had to be returned to the store. Jay-Jay seemed to accept it. But he couldn't get the mattresses to fit so easily. In the end, the back hatch had to be tied shut with rope. I don't know how Grady had accomplished it so easily.

Maybe he had practice from packing vans in his landscaping days.

All this time, I wondered how Grady managed to make such a mess of his life that it threatened to drag his only real friend and his pregnant wife down with him. He wasn't a bad person. This Kitkat guy was probably just taking advantage of Grady's weaknesses. Princess had said Kitkat was doing the mattresses. She said Grady had been hanging out with Kitkat. We should just find Kitkat and give the mattresses to him. But if we did that and got caught somehow, then we would be directly linked to this criminal. On the other hand, if we returned the mattresses to the store and Kitkat found out, he would come after us for the money. I wanted to discuss all this with Princess, but Jay-Jay was sitting next to her on the top of the ramp. She took a fresh pack of Kools from her bag, packed it against her knuckles, and opened it.

"Let me get one," Jay-Jay said.

"You're too young." She lit one and blew smoke at him.

"Yeah, sure," he said. "You're too pregnant."

She took another drag and gave the rest of the cigarette to Jay-Jay. Then she gave him the rest of the pack and her lighter. "Do you want that motorbike, too?"

"Are you kidding?" he said.

"One more job first."

"You're serious?"

"Just one more job," she said, "and it's yours."

———

In the bus, Jay-Jay said, "I know what's going on. You're doing that mattress scam."

We were at a traffic light, just me and the kid and the mattresses in the bus. Princess had said she had terrible sleep because of the mattresses and the sirens, and then she threw in that her Lamaze instructor told her she should rest more. I couldn't question her with the kid hanging around, waiting to earn his motorbike, so I went along with it.

"What mattress scam?" I said to Jay-Jay. "I don't know what you're talking about." The light changed. I drove north on the parkway.

"This is that mattress scam where you switch tags. The Cody's scam, the one Dorian was doing before he got busted for dealing."

I wasn't about to launch into an argument with Jay-Jay, or ask him who Dorian was. If he knew as much as there being a mattress scam, I knew exactly what I looked like to him. I looked like a crook.

"What do you know about a mattress scam?"

He told me. A guy goes into a Cody's and takes the tags from two down-ticket double mattresses and attaches them to a pair of deluxe queen mattresses. The risk here is getting caught in the act of switching. If it's discovered at the register that the tags are wrong, the switcher can pretend the tags were on the mattress already, and even show revulsion at the actual steep price of a queen mattress. But the cashiers usually just ring up whatever comes across their scan guns. Then the shopper takes the mattresses to another Cody's to return them. If the product is Cody's brand, still in the package, and Cody's still stocks it, it can be returned to any Cody's for a full refund. It's almost two hundred dollars profit per mattress. Jay-Jay had even heard of people borrowing Cody's suits for weddings and funerals. You just have to be careful not to stain anything.

Somewhere in the middle of Jay-Jay's lecture, it hit home. I'd been suckered into knowingly committing a crime that Grady had me doing blind only a day earlier. I agreed only because I felt trapped, as though those mattresses had pinned me to the floor, and Princess and Jay-Jay had put them on top of me, and only those two could free me. I was being manipulated.

"I'm wondering how you know about all these schemes," I said. "Know what I think? You're a thief."

"You're calling *me* a thief?" He laughed. "You gotta be fucking kidding me."

"You stole those bicycles. You were riding two different bicycles yesterday, and you showed up right when Princess or Anne needed someone to help her."

"Yeah, great detective work." He lit one of the cigarettes she'd given him. "I didn't ask for this job."

"I gave her my address," I said. "She asked for it before she went back in the diner to pee, but she really went back to the diner to call you."

"I think the heat's getting to you," he said. "Maybe you watch too many cop shows."

I turned east on Montauk Highway. "Don't smoke in my bus." I rolled his window down.

In the short silence that followed, nothing I had said made sense to me anymore. Princess didn't know Jay-Jay before yesterday. I was being defensive. I was blaming my misfortune on a kid. And then I started worrying about him being a kid. He was underage, and I was taking him to rip off a department store.

"Oh, fuck," was all I had to say. The store was coming up on the left.

It was the longest three hours of my life, driving from Cody's to Cody's, waiting for the return of the minor I sent into the store to swipe hundreds in cash. Some of that money was Grady's. Maybe the hundred and forty he owed me was mixed in. Maybe Kitkat thought all this money was his.

It was my idea to drop off at four different Cody's. I also skipped the Cody's where Grady was arrested, going all the way to Freeport to unload the last one. Jay-Jay slept between drop-offs. Either he'd been up all night or he was so used to this variety of criminal activity that it bored him. I'd nudge him awake, he'd take the bandana off, pull a mattress out, and wheel it into the store on a shopping cart. Then he'd come back and give me the cash. We talked only to confirm that no one at the store seemed suspicious.

"Those people are zombies," Jay-Jay said. "Their job sucks."

"That's the problem," I said. "They might be looking for excitement. Catching a thief might be fun for them."

"Are you going to keep doing that? Really?"

"I'm the thief," I said. "I was talking about me."

We got back to the cottage around the time people were coming home from the beach to avoid twilight mosquitoes. The boat was gone from the yard. Meredith's car was gone, and her phone was ringing. Princess was gone, too, but her things were still in my cottage. She left a note, along with keys and papers for the motorbike.

> Dear Michael. I went to work. I'll be back. Don't panic. Here are papers and keys for motorbike for JJ payment minus two bikes. Leave two bikes for Bethany boys for future when bigger. Give Sal $550 for boat. Shift ends at ten. Pick me up.

"Who's Sal?" Jay-Jay said.

"The landlady's son."

Jay-Jay grabbed the keys and papers. He went outside.

"Where are you going?"

He got on the motorbike. He tried the key. I watched from the top of the ramp. There was a feeble whine from the starter. He tried again. Nothing. He got on his red bicycle and pedaled away.

"Wait!" I said. "My seats!" But he kept going.

I wanted to believe that if the seats were in the bus, all this business would be over, but I still had Princess's stuff. I had her money, most of it Sal's now. Why did she buy his boat? Was she going to do Lamaze classes? Who would be her partner? Did she have a place to stay?

She got off at ten. We'd figure out the bus seats then. I needed a shower.

Later, Sal knocked on my door. He's a nurse who goes to patients' homes, mostly old people who can't get around much on their own. There are similarities to our jobs. We're both driving all the time. I can recognize his car on the highway. When he comes to someone's house, he talks to them the way a nurse might talk to his elderly patients, with the volume turned up.

"Hi, Michael," Sal said. "How are you feeling today?"

"Sal. Oh, I have money for you. Money for the boat." I wheeled back, and he came in.

"I actually came over to help you with your seats before," he said. "You were out. Lucky day, though! I've been thinking about selling that boat."

"Do you know why she bought it?"

"I didn't ask. I just took my opportunity. Did you say you have the money?"

"You trusted her?" I said.

"My mom knows Anne since birth. My mom was Anne's mother's Lamaze instructor."

I counted out the money for the boat. I had a hundred and forty dollars left over.

Meredith called from across the yard. "Are you over there, Sal? Is my son over there? I want to tell you what I just heard. There was a crime in the neighborhood."

"Smashed windows," Meredith said.

We were out on the ramp. The sun coasted the horizon.

"What did you hear?" Sal said.

"It was where the Monroes used to live."

"Who lives there now?"

"I don't know. Someone broke a girl's bedroom window, and all the windows in the dining room. This area is getting bad."

"It's everywhere," Sal said. "Did you hear what else happened? There were two arrests at the Cody's in Bellport. First, the police arrested a black guy they initially only wanted to question. They were looking for a man and a woman who burgled a pharmacy of its cigarettes. Cartons and cartons of cigarettes. These people drove a stolen truck into the front window and took all the cigarettes. The black guy kept putting his hands out toward the cop, and the cop felt threatened, so he asked the man to turn around and put his hands on the car. This was for his own safety. But the black guy's girlfriend came out because she was getting off work. She was hysterical right away, asking the cops why they were harassing her man."

"'Why you harassing my man?'" Meredith said. She swiveled her head and wagged her finger. "I can just see it," she said. "'You harassing my man?' Why was he sitting in the parking lot?"

"Maybe he was picking her up," I said.

"And you know what happened at the gas station?" Meredith said.

"Yeah, but then," Sal said, "the guy turns around while they're trying to subdue the girl, and now they have to wrestle him to the ground. The police only wanted to question these people. Now they got them on all kinds of charges. And I think the guy was a dealer. He had pot on him. That's what people are saying. We still don't know if they stole those cigarettes."

"Didn't another guy get arrested at Cody's?" I said.

"What for?"

"For shoplifting?"

"I didn't hear about that," Sal said. "I guess it wasn't a serious crime compared to the other one, so no one's talking about it. Where did you hear about shoplifting? Oh, wait. The police were there for a disturbance before they made this other arrest. Maybe that was it."

"That could be," I said.

"Why you harassing, man?" the younger of the two boys said to the older one. They were playing where the boat used to be.

"No," said the older boy, "it goes, 'You harassing my man?'" He was trying to teach his brother to be funny.

Meredith's phone rang.

"You harassing, my man?" the younger one said.

"Hey, time for hot dogs," Meredith said to the boys. And then she led them inside and answered her phone. I imagine she was receiving more details about the broken windows, maybe about the gas station incident.

"And did you hear about what happened in the diner?" Sal said.

"What happened? What diner?"

"The police," he said. "There was an arrest."

"When, today?"

"No, yesterday. It was a fake arrest. It turned out to be a marriage proposal."

Jay-Jay came riding along the fence on the red bicycle, pulling the blue bike along in tandem.

"Here comes someone," Sal said. "Anyway, it worked. The woman said yes. I love when stuff like that happens."

Jay-Jay rode up on the driveway, guiding both bikes around my minibus. He got off and leaned the bikes against the side of my ramp, and then turned and walked back down the drive and out the gate. He grabbed the motorbike by the handlebars, rocked it off the kickstand, and started walking it away.

"What was that all about?" Sal said, again using his louder nursing voice.

Jay-Jay stopped and turned around. "Are you asking me?"

"Sure."

"Those bikes are for the kids. The two kids. Bethany's kids."

"Really?" Sal said. "And where did you come from?"

"Up the block and around the corner."

"And you're just giving them bicycles?"

"They're for the future," Jay-Jay said. "When the boys are bigger."

"When they're bigger," Sal said. "Okay. And that's your motorbike?"

"Why?"

"I just figured someone dumped it there. I didn't think it belonged to anyone. Do you want to sell it? I can pay cash, or we can trade something. Help me put the seats back in Michael's bus, and we'll talk about it."

When the seats were in, Sal and Jay-Jay agreed on a time and place to meet about trading the motorbike for a Caprice Classic Sal had just got running.

All I could do was wait for Princess to get off work. Her shift ended at ten. Everything she owned in the world was in my cottage: the dining set, the lamps, and about thirty boxes. I reached over and nudged a stack. They were lighter than books or clothes. Something encased in packing foam?

I forgot to include the boat. That was the other thing Princess had in her possession. A dining set, lamps, those boxes, and a boat.

The box atop the stack on the coffee table had been opened at one end. The tape had come loose, or it had been pulled loose and stuck back on. I peeled it back again. I opened the box. It was packed full of cartons of Kools, one carton short. The next box was full of boxed Marlboros. She had Camels, Newports, Parliaments, Winstons—all of them.

I did my handgrip exercises in the bus while I waited for ten p.m. I should have been doing my grip exercises all along, and pull-ups, and taking strolls. It's hard to keep those habits up when you spend most of your time driving.

I didn't know what I was going to say to Anne—to Princess. Did she and Grady rob a pharmacy? Was the furniture stolen, too? What was the boat for? Maybe she already had a buyer, five hundred profit. A guy with a dozen children had been stockpiling them in his yard. Boats are a kind of currency around here.

Maybe she was the one doing the mattresses all along.

Princess, or Anne, or Kitkat never came out of the diner. At ten thirty, I rolled in and took the booth with a view of the door. There were people like me in there at that hour, some of them trying to finish an order too big for them to eat, others overcaffeinated, all of us alone at our booths. I ordered coffee from a different waitress. She guessed Princess wasn't working there anymore. Princess never showed for her shift.

I knew then that, by the time I got home, all her things would be gone. It was almost midnight. I ordered another coffee and sat for a spell longer, watching the clock above the door, waiting for the hands to carry us all into Monday.

Acknowledgments

The influences behind the conception of this book are varied and span decades. Foremost, I am deeply indebted to Zachary Lazar, a great mentor and friend since my first workshop at Hofstra University in 1998. *Floyd Harbor* exists owing to his unwavering advocacy.

At Catapult, Pat Strachan's perceptive questions and deft strokes of the pencil brought this collection into sharper focus. I couldn't have hoped for a better editor. Thanks also to Andy Hunter, John McGhee, and Alisha Gorder.

I thank my mother, Mercedes Maria, who can spin simple narrative from the chaos of life. My father, Peter Joseph, showed me a thing or two about character and voice. His memory lives in a few of these stories. For the love and drama, thanks to my siblings—Peter, Tricia, Sean, Eric,

Adriel, Sheila, Brooke, Matthew, Brianne, and Brittany—may she rest in peace. I'm grateful, too, for the fellowship with the other writers in my family, my sister Shannon and her husband, Adam Penna.

Thanks to the long-defunct Regional Alternative High School in Oakdale for the second chances, John Flanagan for his impassioned classroom readings, my friend Renee Carrick for daring me to write, and Jon Hawkins for supporting my earliest attempts at Suffolk County Community College. The University of Michigan provided the opportunity for me to grow under the exceptional guidance of Peter Ho Davies, Laura Kasischke, Eileen Pollack, and Thomas Lynch, and with the invaluable camaraderie of my fellow MFAers. Thanks especially to Elizabeth Ames Staudt and Todd Myles Carnam for their enduring encouragement.

My Lithuanian family has supported my writing in myriad ways. I am particularly appreciative to Danielius and Rimgaudas Vaitkus for the free office services. Finally, most of these stories would have had awful titles if not for my wife and first reader, Simona Vaitkute. Thanks for your insight, for expanding my horizons, and for Oskar. *Aš tave myliu.*